DEEP COVER

A Harry Vicary Mystery - the second novel in a brand-new crime series set in London from the author of the Hennessey and Yellich mysteries

When the snow thaws on London's Hampstead Heath after a harsh winter, a ghoulish discovery is made that marks the start of a very dangerous case for Detective Inspector Harry Vicary and his team. A body of a man is found on top of a shallow grave containing the battered remains of a young woman. He appears to have frozen to death - but what is his connection to the remains below? Vicary's investigation leads him deep into London's criminal underworld...

DEEP COVER

A Harry Vicary Novel

Peter Turnbull

Severn House Large Print
London & New York

This first large print edition published 2013
in Great Britain and the USA by
SEVERN HOUSE PUBLISHERS LTD of
19 Cedar Road, Sutton, Surrey, England, SM2 5DA.
First world regular print edition published 2011 by
Severn House Publishers Ltd., London and New York.

British Library Cataloguing in Publication Data

Turnbull, Peter, 1950- author.
  Deep cover. -- Large print edition. -- (A Harry Vicary
  mystery ; 2)
  1. Vicary, Harry (Fictitious character)--Fiction.
  2. Police--England--London--Fiction. 3. Murder--
  Investigation--England--London--Fiction. 4. Detective
  and mystery stories. 5. Large type books.
  I. Title II. Series
  823.9'2-dc23

ISBN-13: 9780727896513

Severn House Publishers support the Forest Stewardship
Council™ [FSC™], the leading international forest certification
organisation. All our titles that are printed on FSC certified paper
carry the FSC logo.

Printed and bound in Great Britain by
T J International, Padstow, Cornwall.

PROLOGUE

Two men stood at the edge of a stand of shrubs on Hampstead Heath at the edge of Ken Wood. The recent fall of snow had, for the most part, covered the body beside which the two men stood. Wind sliced across the Heath, carrying with it a fine drizzle from a low, grey sky. The men shivered. One pulled his coat collar up against the rain. The other stamped his feet to improve the circulation. It was early afternoon, yet lights burned in the offices and homes in London, surrounding the Heath with a shimmering ring of yellow and white light.

'Strange place to lie down and die.' 'Mongoose Charlie' cleared his throat and spat the yellow phlegm into the crisp snow beside him. 'Strange old place.'

'Saved us a job though.' Sydney Pilcher blew into his hands. 'Saved us a right job.' Pilcher then turned and walked across the snow in a slow, deliberate manner, retracing his steps back towards Spaniards Road.

'Mongoose Charlie' remained by the corpse for a few seconds. Then he turned and followed Pilcher. 'You're right, boss,' he said softly, 'he saved us a right old job.'

ONE

It was 'that' winter. It was caused, the meteorologists announced, by a high-pressure cell that was stationary over Iceland and had thus allowed the arctic weather to sweep south and over the entire United Kingdom with a substantial blanket of snow and ice, especially black ice. It was further reported that the winter was the coldest winter for twenty years, and it came at a price. There was an endless stream of walking wounded who inundated the accident and emergency departments of the country's hospitals, mainly suffering from fractures caused by slipping while walking on the unseen ice or from slow impact car accidents, but accidents that were sufficiently serious to cause non-fatal injuries. All of which had to be treated. There were also the inevitable fatalities, some very tragic, like the young man found floating in the pool of a water fountain dressed only in a tee shirt and denim jeans, who had died of drowning brought on by hypothermia and alcohol excess. Other incidents had an amusing quality, such as the one wherein two youths had driven their car far along the surface of an iced-over canal until, inevitably, they had encountered a patch of thinner ice and their car had plunged into three feet of water. Then had come the thaw, and, when it came, it brought with it its own unique set of problems: flooded homes in the main, and the discovery of bodies of people who had been reported missing at the height of the snowy weather. The body of a man called Michael Dalkeith being one such.

Michael Dalkeith's body was discovered lying face down in the mud by a dog walker who was immediately touched by the spectacle; the poignancy reached her, deeply so. The woman noticed that the man wore clothing which was wholly inadequate for the weather. She saw a battered and torn wax-coated jacket, she saw denim jeans, which she knew from experience offered no protection against the cold, especially when aggravated by wind chill, and further aggravated, in this case, by the fact that they were clearly old, faded and threadbare, and which had ridden up his left leg to reveal that the wretched man was without thermal underwear and wore only short cotton socks and running shoes. Clothing suited only to warm, autumnal evenings, so thought the dog walker. He did not even have gloves upon his hands. The deceased had black hair and grimy looking skin, and he appeared to the woman to be a lowlife, most likely a street beggar, she thought, though he seemed to be older than most beggars she was used to seeing. But no one, not anyone, deserved this; dying alone in a snowstorm on the Heath, such a short distance from some of the most valuable houses in London, surrounded by wealth and warmth.

The woman slipped the lead round the neck of her King Charles spaniel and led him gently away from the body. She surveyed the scene before her as she walked to Spaniards Road; evergreen foliage had emerged with the thaw and a clear blue sky overlooked London, although the wind still blew keenly from the east. At Spaniards Road the dog walker halted and addressed a young man in a duffel coat who was about to enter the park, asking him whether he possessed 'One of those damn mobile things? You know those little boxes that people hold to their ear and ruin everyone's railway journeys?'

The man grinned at the woman's indignation and took out a mobile phone from his jacket pocket. 'One of these?' he asked.

'Yes ... loathsome things. Phone the police, can you?'

'Yes,' the man replied, a curious note having entered his voice, 'I can. Why should I?'

'Well, do so. Why? Because there's a body over there.' The woman turned and pointed towards Ken Wood.

'Can you show me?' the man asked.

'I'd rather you call the police. I don't like indulging ghoulish behaviour.'

'I am one.'

'A ghoul!'

The man smiled. 'No, I am a police officer, off duty, but then a policeman is never off duty, not officially. Just show me, please.' The wind tugged at the man's hair.

Upon being shown the body, the police officer dialled 999 and gave his location and reason for calling. He took note of the dog walker's name and address and then remained in attendance.

So much, he thought, for his first day off in many, many weeks. There is no justice in life and there's no rest for the wicked. There just isn't.

The white-haired man sat back in the deep, leather-covered armchair and pulled strongly on a large Havana cigar, and then ex-

10

haled, blowing neat smoke circles as he did so. 'Well, now we know where the little toerag went and he won't be doing us no harm. Pity though, I wanted him to have a slap or two, but at least he's gone, that's the main thing.'

The woman smiled but remained silent and glanced out of the tall rear windows of the house on to the back lawn and the woods beyond, as the sun exploited a gap in the cloud cover and shone down through the drizzle, creating what she called 'damp sunshine'.

'See, toerags like that toerag, they're not up to much ... they don't count for much, they never amount to much ... but it's toerags like that little toerag that know where all the bodies are buried, and it's that which makes them dangerous. But now we know where he went: he went for a walk on Hampstead Heath and then he went for a kip in the snow.'

'Neat.' The woman returned her gaze to the man and did so adoringly. 'That's neat. I am pleased with you.'

Five minutes after he made the phone call, the off-duty police officer heard the siren of the approaching police vehicle, and, as the white car with its blue lights flashing ap-

11

proached him, he raised his hand. The car stopped beside him and two young uniformed constables got out of the vehicle.

'Deceased person in the shrubs.' The man showed his ID.

'Yes, sir,' the driver replied.

'This isn't my patch ... I am off duty, allegedly. Come, I'll show you.' He replaced his ID in his jacket pocket and, with the two constables walking immediately behind him, led the way up the slippery grassy slope to the edge of Ken Wood and showed them the corpse. 'It's clammy to the touch,' he explained. 'I'm no medical man but he is dead alright. The snow must have preserved the flesh to some extent. Found by a dog walker. I have her details for you. It's your pigeon now but I can't see any suggestion of suspicious circumstances. Looks like a down-and-out who went to sleep in the snow ... but like I said, it's your pigeon.'

'We're finding a few like him, sir, once the snow melts it's the same each winter.'

'Yes, I know, so are we. All London is finding bodies.'

The constable grasped the radio which was attached to his lapel and contacted his control, requesting a police surgeon and CID in attendance. His calm, unhurried manner impressed the off-duty officer. The constable then took note of the officer's name and contact details, and also the details of the dog walker who'd found the body. 'People say they like a good hard and long frost, it kills off sickly vegetation–' he closed his notebook – 'but they don't think about sickly human beings.'

'Indeed.' The off-duty officer turned and looked over the Heath, down towards Parliament Hill. 'Red Kite!'

'Sorry, sir?'

'Red Kite ... that bird ... see it? That's a Red Kite, they're scavengers. I had a pheasant in my garden a week or two ago, strutting up and down like he was the cock of the walk. I came for a breath of fresh air and a chance to observe some of inner London's wildlife, of which there is much, not quite as exotic as the vultures in New York City, but interesting just the same.'

'Yes, sir.'

'Well, you don't need me any more. I'll go and rescue what I can from my day off.'

Harry Vicary halted his car behind the vehicles already parked in a restricted area on Spaniards Hill, close to the entrance of the Heath. He saw police vehicles, a black, windowless mortuary van, two unmarked cars, all supervised by a solitary woman police officer, there to move curious pedestrians on and to legitimize the parking of the vehicles in the 'No Parking' area. Vicary left his car and walked up to the WPC. 'Detective Inspector Vicary' – he showed her his ID – 'I was asked to attend here.'

'Yes, sir.' The WPC spoke with a distinct Scottish accent. 'Up there, sir.' She pointed to the wooded area and then Vicary saw the police activity: uniformed officers, a white and blue tape strung from shrub to shrub and a white inflatable tent. He identified John Shaftoe and Detective Constable Ainsclough, and walked laboriously up the slope, stopping to tuck the bottom of his trousers into his socks, caring not about the image he presented by doing so. As he approached the focus of activity DC Ainsclough separated himself from the group and walked towards Vicary.

'More than a frozen corpse, sir,' Ainsclough advised.

'Oh?'

'Yes, sir.' Ainsclough seemed to Vicary to be nervous of authority, which Vicary always interpreted as being a healthy sign; far, far preferable in his view to arrogant individuals who seem to feel they are everyone's equal, if not their superior.

'Seems so, sir,' Ainsclough stammered,

'...frankly I would not have noticed it, but Mr Shaftoe was keen-eyed.'

'So what have we got?'

'I'll show you, sir.' Ainsclough led Vicary to the place where the frozen corpse was found and where John Shaftoe was already standing. Upon reaching the spot, Vicary nodded to Shaftoe and the two men whispered a brief 'Hello' to each other.

'Here, sir.' Ainsclough pointed to the ground. Vicary saw only ground, loose soil and a few clumps of sodden grass, recently exposed by the thaw. 'I'm sorry—' he turned to Shaftoe – 'what am I looking at?'

'Look carefully, the man's head was close to the laurel bush ... his feet are where we are standing ... say six feet between the bush and ourselves.'

'I still...'

'Now look at the ground upon which we stand and behind us...'

Vicary did so. 'Mud and grass,' he said. 'What you'd expect on the Heath.'

'And consolidated.' Shaftoe grinned. 'Yet here, with shrubs on three sides to conceal it, and a fourth side, narrow so as to serve as an entrance. All the ground herein is disturbed.' Shaftoe was barrel-chested, with a ruddy complexion and wispy white hair. 'Still don't see it?' His short stature obliged

15

him to look up at Vicary.

'No...' Vicary shook his head. He was growing deeply more curious because he knew Shaftoe to be a man, a gentleman, a professional, who took his work seriously. He was not, in Vicary's experience, the sort of man to play games. He was not at all the sort of man to summon him from his desk to look at muddy soil on Hampstead Heath. 'Go on, tell me.'

'It's a shallow grave.' Shaftoe spoke calmly. 'I'll lay a pound to your penny that there is a corpse down there. The down-and-out went to sleep over a corpse, possibly a skeleton.'

'Recently dug?'

'Not necessarily, which is why I said possibly a skeleton. It isn't so much the amount of soil that is exposed, that could have been caused by animals ... badgers or foxes scratching at the surface ... it is more the slight raising of the ground, as if the soil has been dug up and replaced over something, and the rectangular nature of the area in question ... roughly rectangular but definitely longer than it is wide and about the dimensions of a human being, an adult human.' Shaftoe paused. 'If I am wrong, I can only apologize for dragging you up here on such an unpleasant day, but I think you

16

ought to undertake an exploratory dig.' Shaftoe paused again and smiled. 'Congratulations on your promotion by the way. I haven't seen you since the Epping Forest murder.'

'Thank you. Haven't stitched the stripes on yet, but thank you.'

'I was sorry to hear about Archie Dew.'

'Yes, he is missed. I call on his widow occasionally. She is soldiering on. Manfully is probably the wrong word but I can't think of the right one.'

'No matter, I know what you mean.'

'So,' Vicary brought the conversation back to the matter in hand, 'we have one death, most likely by misadventure...'

'Yes, sir.' Ainsclough spoke. 'Death was confirmed by the police surgeon and so I requested the pathologist ... and it was when we removed the corpse...'

'Presently in the tent?' Shaftoe nodded to the white inflatable tent that had been erected close to the shrubs. 'Couldn't erect it over the body,' he added. 'No room.'

'I see.'

'It was then that Mr Shaftoe looked at the ground over which the body had lain and said there's something else down there.'

Shaftoe grinned. 'I actually said "Summat's down there", but your man can translate Yorkshire into English.'

'Yorkshire grandfather,' Ainsclough explained.

'I did wonder,' Shaftoe smiled. 'With a name like yours you had to have roots in God's own county.'

'Yes, sir ... but that's when I requested your attendance ... it's more than just a frozen corpse sir, at least it might be.'

'Appears so.' Shaftoe's eye was caught by a 747 flying low over London on its final approach to Heathrow, and watched as the undercarriage was lowered, later than most pilots would have done so by his observations, but the wheels had been lowered and that was the main thing. It was the one thing he always looked for when watching planes land, never having been a passenger on a plane without saying, as the plane approached the ground, 'I hope he's put the wheels down.' He found time to reflect that no one would be talking on the plane at that moment.

'Well ... we'll dig. Can you organize that, DC Ainsclough? We'll be on this all day.'

'Yes, sir.'

'Suggest you clear the shrubs either side of the grave, if it is a grave; moving a down-and-out a few feet from where he slept his final sleep is one thing, but we'll want the tent over a shallow grave.'

'Yes, sir, I'm on it.'

'And get the scene of crime officers here, we'll need photographs.'

'Yes, sir.'

'Can I see the corpse, please?' Vicary turned to Shaftoe.

'Of course,' Shaftoe turned and led the way.

In the tent Vicary considered the body. It said to him poverty. It said low-skilled, possibly unemployed; it said scratching pennies. It did not say down-and-out. It was too clean and did not have the unshaven face and matted hair he had expected. 'Have the pockets been searched?'

'No,' Shaftoe replied. 'Not been touched. No reason not to have him conveyed to the London Hospital to await a post-mortem, but we became sidetracked by the suspicious appearance of the ground on which he lay.'

'I see.'

'I can have him removed, the mortuary van is standing by, but I'd like to stay for the excavation in case what is buried is what I think it is.'

'I'd like you to stay as well, sir,' Vicary replied in a serious manner, 'and for the same reason.'

Ninety minutes later Vicary and Shaftoe stood side by side; adjacent to them stood Ainsclough, and beside him the two officers who had first cleared the shrubs and then had dug down, carefully so, until the Heath gave up its dead.

'Female.' Shaftoe broke the silence that had descended on the small group. 'Remnants of clothing visible ... shoes ... the metal of the high heels is clear to see.'

'So, one for us,' Vicary commented.

'Oh, yes, I'm afraid so, much less than seventy years old ... the burial I mean. The corpse appears to be that of a young ... youngish person.'

'Alright, once the body has been photographed we'll remove it to the London Hospital. I assume you'll be doing the post-mortem, Mr Shaftoe?'

'Yes, I like to follow through whenever possible. Will you be attending for the police?'

Vicary nodded slowly. 'Yes, and for exactly the same reason. I like to follow through as well. It keeps the thread in my mind, keeps it intact and alive.'

Detective Constable Ainsclough stood silently in the ante room next to the mortuary of the London Hospital on Whitechapel

20

Road and pulled on a pair of latex gloves. In front of him, on a table, was the clothing which had been removed from the man who had apparently lain down to die in his sleep in the snow on Hampstead Heath. The clothing had been laid neatly with clear reverence rather than dumped hastily on the table, and Ainsclough approached his task with similar reverence. Taking the wax jacket first, he felt the outside of the pockets for an indication of content, if any, therein and then probed each pocket gently with his fingertips, knowing that drug addicts' needles are small, easily concealed and potentially deadly. He knew personally of one police officer who groped into a youth's pocket during an arrest and search, pricked his finger on something sharp and rapidly withdrew his hand to find his index finger seeping blood. The youth had leered and said, 'I'm positive ... and so are you now.' In the event the HIV test proved negative, but the time that elapsed before the results were known was measured in many a sleepless night for the man, and it was a period of great strain upon his marriage. In this case, a search of the pockets of the jacket revealed nothing more than a set of house keys, just two keys held together with string, and the left rear pocket of the jeans contained a

21

DSS signing-on card at the office in Palmers Green. That was the contents of the man's pockets, two keys and a signing-on card. No money, not even a small amount of coinage; no identity save for a creased white card which gave his status as 'unemployed' and a signing-on date, a number and also his National Insurance number. Ainsclough pondered the man's clothing: a wax jacket (without lining), a shirt, a vest, denim jeans (worn and threadbare), a pair of briefs, a pair of socks (cotton) and a pair of running shoes (well-worn with a split across the sole of the right shoe), and dressed thusly he had wandered on to a heathland in a snow-storm. Eclipsed, thought Ainsclough, just did not describe the man's life. He replaced the clothing in a productions bag labelled so far with only a case number.

He peeled off the latex gloves and dropped them into the 'sin bin' provided from where they would be collected for incineration. He took the clothing in the production bag with him, by car, across London to New Scotland Yard and logged it in as evidence.

When he reached his desk on the Murder and Serious Crime Unit floor, he sat down and picked up the phone in one movement, and called the Department of Social Security office in Palmers Green. He identified himself and his reason for calling, and had the impression his call was being passed from one internal phone to another, until a man with a heavy West Indian accent finally assured Ainsclough that he could be of assistance, but only if he could call him back to verify his identity. Ainsclough gave his name and extension number and sat back and waited for his call to be returned. He glanced out of his office window, which faced west, away from the river, and relished the view of cluttered government buildings, grey and solidly built, and with small, efficient businesslike windows wherein few humans were ever to be seen. Moments later his phone warbled. He let it ring twice before picking it up. 'DC Ainsclough.'

'My man...' The West Indian voice was powerful and warm. 'DSS Palmers Green.'

'Thanks for calling back.'

'I brought his name up on the computer, that signing number, I mean, and his NI number, and both came back with a claimant by the name of Michael Dalkeith.' The DSS officer spelled the surname for Ainsclough. 'Thirty-seven years of age.'

'Thirty-seven?'

'Yes, boss ... thirty-seven summers he has.'

'I thought he looked younger.'

'Lucky man. I could do with looking

younger.'

'Possibly, but you wouldn't want to be in this geezer's shoes, not even if it meant looking younger.'

'Hey man, let me tell you ... this job is the pits, the pay is no better than the benefit given to the claimants. After travel costs we got less to spend on our bellies than the claimants, but I still wouldn't swop places with any one of them ... so maybe he's not so lucky.'

'Well, he's deceased so his luck's out. Good or bad, he has no luck any more.'

'So he'll not be signing this week...' The man laughed softly.

Ainsclough found himself annoyed by the man's callous humour but then reflected on the grinding thankless nature of his job ... poor pay, low morale ... it was not dissimilar to the gallows humour developed by the emergency services. It helps one to survive difficult and often unpleasant forms of employment. 'Well, if he does sign on saying he's lost his card, let us know, we have an identity to confirm.'

'Yes, man, will do, he signs Thursdays ... two p.m.'

'So I saw. Do you have an address?'

'Yes, it's 297 The Crest. Quite posh. We don't get a lot of customers from The Crest;

24

not a lot of custom at all from The Crest, boss man.'

'Has he been signing on for a long time?'

'Not here ... not with us. Just a couple of months with us but he was signing at the Kilburn office for a few years before then, according to his details. Got a previous address...'

'Yes, please, we need to trace any next of kin; can't use the signing-on card as a definite means of identification.'

'OK, boss, got the pen? Got the paper? It was Claremont Road, Kilburn, did well to get from there to The Crest, Palmers Green ... he's still only a doley though.'

'Number?' Ainsclough again found himself getting irritated with the DSS official's jocularity.

'One hundred and twenty-three, single claimant there, but at The Crest he claimed for a partner and two children. He got his little self hitched ... there's your old next of kin, captain.'

'Well, we'll see what we see.' Ainsclough replaced the phone gently and reached for a new blank manila file, in which he entered the information he had just received. He closed the file and placed it in his 'out' tray, pending filing. Michael Dalkeith, unemployed, one of a half a dozen bodies found across London, revealed by the thaw. He got up and walked down the CID corridor to the office which Frankie Brunnie shared with Penny Yewdall. He stood in the doorway, and when Brunnie looked up at him, Ainsclough smiled and said, 'Fancy a trip to Palmers Green?'

Brunnie glanced out of the window at the overcast sky and replied, 'Not really.'

'Poor you.'

Brunnie dropped his pen on to the statistic forms he was completing. 'Poor, poor me but anything is better than monthly stats.'

'I'm impressed; I haven't looked at my December stats yet.'

'These are October's.' Brunnie stood and reached for his coat. 'Nothing to be impressed about, I assure you.'

'Oh, in that case...'

'"Oh" is right. Vicary is not best pleased, nor is he overly impressed with little me, but he's busy with a skeleton right now, or so I hear. So yes, Palmers Green it is.'

'Yes, he won't be back today. I need to ID a stiff, nothing suspicious, just an ID to make, then we can pass the parcel to the family, or the coroner.'

Clive Sherwin looked around him. Never really happy in the country, he felt even less comfortable than usual. The winter-tilled fields beyond the meadow seemed unwelcoming, the leafless trees in the nearby wood at that moment were home to cawing rooks, as the first sliver of dawn cracked the night sky. The three young women had hoods over their heads and each was trembling violently. Sherwin could not tell whether they were shivering with fear, or shivering because of the cold, all three being ill-clad for the weather. But, probably, he thought, it was because of both. They stood at the bottom of a meadow and to their right was a line of cherry trees. The furthest of the trees were tall and established, the nearest of the trees were little more than saplings. There were ten in all. In spring they would develop a blossom of brilliant pink, thus heralding the approach of summer.

'Alright, girls,' the hard-faced woman said quietly, 'take off the hoods.'

The three young women slowly and reluctantly tugged the hoods from their heads. One of the women screamed, all stepped backwards and turned their heads away.

'Scream all you like,' the woman said, 'there's no one to hear you. But look in the hole. Look!'

Clive Sherwin stood a short distance away holding the spade and with a sapling of

27

flowering cherry at his feet. He knew what was in the hole, and he knew what was going to be planted over it, once he had filled it in.

'She was lucky.' The hard-faced woman pointed to the hole. 'She was banged on the head. She was dead when she was put in, on account of her being only fifteen or sixteen, but most times we truss 'em up and bury them alive. Isn't that right, Clive?'

Sherwin nodded but remained silent.

'Most of the time they're alive and know what's happening to them. But we was merciful with her, so we was. Trouble with her, she was skimming. That is naughty. That is well out of order. We picked her up where we found you, on the Embankment ... a runaway ... like you, from up North she was; gave her a roof, gave her food, sent her out to King's Cross to earn her keep. She earned alright, but she didn't hand it all in, kept some dosh for herself. Heard we found out and tried to scarper ... but you can't ... you can't run for ever, not from the firm. We got eyes on every street corner in the smoke, like twenty-four seven. This is what happens if you skim and run. So learn. See all those trees? There's a body under every one of them. And this is the new orchard. The old orchard got full up. So don't be naughty.

Don't get too left field. Don't get out of order. Right, Clive, fill it in.'

Sherwin spaded the soil back into the hole and then planted the cherry tree shrub on top.

'On with your hoods.' The woman barked the order. 'We'll get you back to your drum, you'll be working tonight. You'll need rest and a little food.'

John Shaftoe pulled the anglepoise arm that was bolted into the ceiling above the dissecting table downwards, until the microphone at the end of the arm was level with his mouth. He glanced at Vicary who stood, as protocol dictated, at the edge of the post-mortem laboratory, observing for the police, and was to approach the dissecting table only when invited. He was silent and quite still, and dressed, as required, in green disposable coveralls, with a matching hat and slippers.

'It's always damn same.' Shaftoe adjusted the microphone. Shaftoe spoke with a distinct Yorkshire accent and Vicary noticed, once again, how he omitted the definite article in keeping with the speech pattern of his roots. He would never invite any observing police officer to the dissecting table to view something of forensic significance by saying, 'Come to the table and look at this', it would rather be: 'Come to table'. 'It's Dykk,' Shaftoe continued, 'and cursed am I to work under him and he took dislike to me from day one. Have you ever met him?'

'Yes,' Vicary replied softly, though his voice carried easily through the hard-surfaced pathology laboratory, 'once or twice. Civilized, I have found, though a little aloof at times.'

'Aloof!' Shaftoe snorted. 'Aloof, that's the understatement of year, Home Counties toff who thinks that folk what live north of Watford are all Neanderthals. Well, he lives up to his name. A complete dick and one of his little games is to push the microphone up out of my reach, well, as near as he can when he's finished his body butchering, but he's a professor and I am not. He's a southerner and I am not.' He paused and glared at Button, his mortuary assistant, who just then allowed instruments to clatter needlessly, noisily on to the trolley, and he held the pause as if to say, 'And I've got Button for my assistant and he has not.'

'Sorry, Mr Shaftoe, sir.' Billy Button turned to Shaftoe and offered his apology in a weak and whiny voice, and then turned away again and began to place the instruments neatly on the surface of the trolley.

Shaftoe looked at Vicary and raised his eyebrows. Vicary shrugged his shoulders and smiled in mute response.

'Can you give this a reference number please, Cynthia,' Shaftoe spoke into the microphone, clearly for the hearing of an audio typist who would shortly be typing up the notes on the post-mortem, 'and also today's date? The body is fully skeletonized and is of the female sex, and Northern European or possibly Asian in terms of racial extraction.' He turned to Vicary. 'Have to be careful, those two races have similar skeletons. In general, Asians are more finely boned, but nonetheless, each can be mistaken for the other.' He returned to the corpse. 'The rich soils of Hampstead saw to that. The damp soil, full of micro-organisms, all feasting on the flesh, you see, and complete skeletonization in those conditions could be achieved within ten years, but strangely not disturbed by the foxes and badgers which live on the Heath. Mind you, the burial site was near a footpath, which, in turn, was quite near Spaniards Road; probably too much street lighting and traffic noise to make them feel safe, they'd be happier deeper in the Heath.'

Vicary nodded. 'Yes, that would probably explain it. I confess, it's not at all my area of

31

expertise but I did wonder why the grave hadn't been disturbed by scavengers, especially when I saw how shallow it was.'

'Indeed ... well ... skeletons do not tell us as many tales as a fresh corpse would, but they tell us sufficient ... and this lady died of a fractured skull.' Shaftoe ran his latex encased fingertips over the surface of the deceased's skull. 'Of note is a single massive blow to the top of the head which is linear in form. Care to take a look?'

Vicary stepped forward and approached the dissecting table. He examined the top of the skull and noted the linear depression with minor fractures leading from it.

'That,' Shaftoe said with a restrained, matter-of-fact tone, 'is what's called making sure. The felon was making sure alright, God in heaven was he making sure. Or she. You don't survive a blow like that, not on this planet anyway.'

'Murder?'

'Oh yes, it's the linear pattern which suggests a blow to the skull with a linear weapon ... a golf club would do nicely. If she had fallen head first on to a hard surface you'd see a more radial pattern of fractures.'

'I see.'

'The blow seems to have landed right on top of her head, which suggests that she was

in a sitting position when she was attacked
... possibly from behind, but that's suppo-
sition. I just say what caused her to stop
breathing, if I can ... and don't ever ask me
the time of death ... not ever. That's the stuff
of television shows. I'll determine her approximate height in a moment, but she is
not going to be a tall woman – about five
foot or one hundred and fifty centimetres.'
He paused. 'Ah ... the wrists have been fractured, and, yes, so have the ankles, as if she
was disabled before being killed. The ankle
and wrist fractures are peri-mortem ... and
two of her ribs have been fractured on her
right side.'

'Battered to death.'

'Well, yes, but the fractured ribs, ankles
and wrists would not be an attempt to kill
her; it's more in the manner of being tortured before being murdered.'

'Strewth!'

'Strewth is right. The work of a very bad
boy or girl ... this is a right bad 'un.'

'All about the same time? I mean, occur-
red at the same time?'

'All peri-mortem, yes.' Shaftoe rested his
stubby fingers on the edge of the stainless
steel table. 'But the fractures to the wrists
and ankles seem to be deliberate, precise.
The blow to the head has the sense of being

33

a single strike at a can't-miss target. So, the overall impression is that she was disabled prior to being murdered.'

Vicary groaned, then inhaled through his nose and received the strong smell of formaldehyde. 'So this is not just a murder victim? It ... she is also a torture victim?'

'Seems so, there is a story here, a right old yarn.'

'Can you tell how old she was at her time of death?'

'Yes, I'll extract a tooth; that will give us her age at death to within twenty-four months, that is to say an age, plus or minus twelve months ... but she was an adult and she had given birth. You note the pelvic scarring? That is caused by breech delivery ... two or more children. I can say that she was over the age of twenty-five when she died. The skull plates have knitted together. There is no indication of rheumatics or arthritis. I accept that children can succumb to infantile arthritis and that is not a funny number, but, by and large, rheumatics and arthritis are indications of middle to old age and are not present.' Shaftoe pointed into the skeleton's mouth. 'British dental work, you'll be able to confirm her identity from her dentures if she was murdered less than eleven years ago. Dentists are obliged by law to keep all records for eleven years after the patient last attended their surgery. Some keep them for longer. I'll detach the skull and send it to the forensic science people, they can use computer generated imagery to produce a likeness ... used to take a week to do that using plasticine ... now it takes seconds.'

'Appreciated.'

'Once that has been done, I'll extract an upper molar and cut it into cross-section; from that I can determine her age within twenty-four months, as I said. Then I'll detach the lower jaw and our forensic odontologist will be able to make a positive or a negative match to any dental records you can send us.'

'Thank you.'

'For your attention at the Yard, Mr Vicary?'

'Yes, please. Seems I am the senior interest officer, for my sins.'

Shaftoe grinned, 'For your sins. So that's it: tortured, murdered, adult female who had given birth. Oh ... and probably Western European ... and too damn young to be in here – mind you, they always are.'

Vicary made his thanks and exited the pathology laboratory.

Moments later, when Shaftoe and Button

were alone in the laboratory, save for the skeleton of the unidentified victim, Shaftoe said, 'Billy...'

'Yes, sir ... I'm sorry, sir,' the slightly built man whimpered.

'Billy, nobody is ever going to call me a pull-yourself-together merchant but you really do need to start mustering some self-control. You can be seen trembling ... it doesn't look good. When we have observing police officers we need to present as calm, competent, professional men, good at our jobs ... and don't dismiss your job lightly, Billy. I could not do mine if you couldn't do thine.'

'Yes, sir ... thank you, sir ... but you see, sir, my sister's cousin died last week and that sort of thing always brings it home, that one day I'll be on that table, being cut open with this scalpel, sir ... by you, sir, or by one of the other gentlemen, sir ... or one of the ladies.' Button looked pleadingly at Shaftoe.

'I've told thee before, Billy,' Shaftoe mustered patience, 'it's highly *un*likely that you'll need to be given a post-mortem examination; you are unlikely to be caring for the instruments that will be used to cut you open. Only suspicious or unknown causes need apply for a place on that table, which is the minority of deaths in the UK.'

'Yes, sir...' Button stammered. 'Can I go now, sir?'

'Yes ... yes...' Shaftoe peeled off the latex gloves and dropped them into the yellow bin in the corner of the laboratory, and once again he reflected that the wretched Button should have taken a job mowing the lawns in the parks in whichever London borough he lived. He then pondered, also as before, that he was better served by the Billy Buttons of this world than by the sort of man who is fascinated by morbidity and is seen to gleam at corpses, or by the necrophiliacs who are not unknown to smooth their way through the vetting process. Nonetheless, Shaftoe accepted that one very square peg in one very round hole did not begin to describe the extent of the mismatch between Billy Button and his job in the pathology laboratory of the London Hospital, EC1.

The woman flung the door open. Two men she did not recognize stood on the threshold. One man was tall, clean-shaven, slender, the other was equally tall, but heavily built with a striking black beard. Both were smartly dressed in plain clothes. She was startled and shut the door a little. The visitors were clearly unexpected. 'Can I help you?' she asked.

'DC Ainsclough.' The slender, clean-shaven one showed the woman his ID. 'This is DC Brunnie.'

Brunnie also showed his ID.

'Police! Is there something the matter?' Behind her, Ainsclough and Brunnie saw a cluttered hallway and heard two children playing noisily. Ainsclough glanced along The Crest, Palmers Green, a neat terrace of two-storey houses with bay windows. No person was on the street, though he noticed a curtain twitch in the downstairs room of an adjacent house.

'We're here in connection with a Mr Dalkeith.'

'He's not here.'

'Yes...' Ainsclough spoke softly. 'We thought he might not be ... but does he live here?'

'Yes.'

'I see. What relationship is he to you, if I may ask?'

'He's my husband ... but he walked out. He left just before Christmas. Imagine that, two children and he walks out just before Christmas. I am Annie Dalkeith.'

'Do you know where he is?'

'He has a room in Kilburn. He told me to forward his mail and like a fool, I do so.' Mrs Annie Dalkeith was a small, round woman with a mop of brown hair. She wore a large pullover and tracksuit bottoms. Her feet were encased in pink slippers.

'Mrs Dalkeith—' Ainsclough glanced along the street – 'we may have some bad news for you and this is a bit public...'

Annie Dalkeith paled, and then stepped aside. 'I haven't tidied up; you take me as you find me.'

'Don't worry.' Ainsclough stepped over the threshold, followed by Brunnie.

Annie Dalkeith shut the door behind the officers and directed them to the living room of the house, which the officers found untidy and chaotic, but not at all unclean. Strangely, the curtains were half-closed, allowing just sufficient daylight into the room so as not to require the light to be switched on, but what light there was seemed to be admitted with a certain reluctance. Annie Dalkeith plucked a large plastic child's toy off the settee and invited the officers to take a seat, while she sat in an armchair and shakily lit a cigarette. The children, still unseen in a nearby room, had stopped squabbling, as if hushed by the sudden presence of strangers in the house.

'Mrs Dalkeith...' Ainsclough struggled, 'we believe that your husband may be deceased.'

'Michael ... oh...'

'Yes. The ... he has still to be identified ... so that will mean—'

'So that's what he meant?' She sat back and drew heavily on the cigarette. 'I did wonder.'

'What do you mean?'

'Well, he left us in December, like I said. He did not say why. He and I hadn't quarrelled ... nothing like that had happened. Ours wasn't a perfect marriage but it was working. What happened?'

'We believe he died of exposure in the recent cold snap.'

'Oh...'

'On Hampstead Heath.'

'On the Heath? Michael knew the Heath. He liked to walk on it. He was a good father but he would never take the children on to the Heath for some reason that he never would explain.'

'Interesting. So tell us, why did you say "So that's what he meant"?'

'Just that he said that he had to leave us for our sakes ... he wouldn't explain. He just said it was for "the best". It wasn't easy for him. He loved the children, loved his beer like any Irishman, but he loved his children more.'

'He was Irish?'

'Yes.'

'With a name like Dalkeith? Sounds Scottish to me.'

'Grandfather, maybe great grandfather was English, a Londoner, and seems he didn't go a whole bunch on the notion of fighting the "People's War" back in 1939 and went to live in Ireland – in the Republic – to avoid being conscripted. Went to Cork, married a local girl and started a family, the Dalkeiths. Michael is third or fourth generation and wanted to return to his family roots in London ... but he was Irish ... Irish parents, grew up in Ireland, thick Irish accent.'

'I see.'

'I've read about Irishmen who came over to volunteer for the London Irish Regiment, and others who joined the navy and the airforce, who pretended to be Ulstermen to join the forces, like Americans who pretended to be Canadians, but I didn't know there was a two-way traffic,' Brunnie commented.

'Apparently, not a few Brits did the same thing in 1939, and Canadians went to live in the USA at the same time and for the same reason, but that's history.'

'Yes...' Ainsclough sat forward. 'Was your husband employed?'

Annie Dalkeith shrugged, 'Odd jobs. He had a bit of a record, but you'll know that.'

'Yes, just petty stuff and nothing recent, but you said he left "for the best". Strange thing to say?'

'Yes.'

'He gave no reason?'

'No ... but he'd been agitated for a while ... sleeping badly.'

'So he was worried about something?'

'Yes, but he never said what. Then, just out of the blue, he said he was leaving us. Oh yes, he said we'd be safe that way.'

'Safe?'

'That's what he said...'

At that moment two small mixed-race children, a boy and a girl, ran into the room, crying 'Mummy, Mummy'. Annie Dalkeith smiled and gathered them into her arms. 'He's their stepfather,' she explained apologetically, 'but he loved them just the same.' She stood and took the children back to the other room.

'Can you accompany us to the London Hospital, please?'

'Now?'

'Yes ... we have to identify the body.'

'The body...' Annie Dalkeith echoed the words. 'The body...'

'Indelicate of me...' Ainsclough stammered. 'I'm sorry.'

'No ... no, it's alright, it's something I will

42

have to get used to. I'll get my coat. Let me go next door, I'll ask Mrs James to watch my children.'

'Could you let us have the address in Kilburn, the one your husband was using?'

'One-two-three Claremont Road,' she tapped the side of her head, 'it's lodged in here ... Kilburn where half of Ireland lives. Funny, when he came to London to look for his roots, he ended up in Little Ireland.'

When Annie Dalkeith had left the house to take her children to her neighbour's, Ainsclough turned to Brunnie, 'There's more to this than misadventure. My waters tell me there's a story here. I want to visit the address in Kilburn if it's a positive identity ... which it will be.'

Brunnie nodded briskly. 'Yes, it sounds ... well ... one copper to another, it sounds interesting.'

Annie Dalkeith declined the offer of a lift home and took the tube back to Palmers Green. She didn't want to be above ground, the tube felt right, it felt correct, it felt appropriate to be rattling through a pitch black tunnel in a carriage where no one spoke – even good friends could not sustain a conversation on an underground train. The silence all around her and the pitch

43

black outside the window seemed to provide the perfect atmosphere in which to contemplate widowhood at just thirty-one years of age.

She left the tube at Southgate and walked slowly home, not wanting to rush the journey, not wanting to collect her two children, not wanting to tell them that 'Mikey' hasn't just gone for a holiday. He had gone, gone ... gone for good ... and not because he doesn't want us. Identifying his body hadn't been like it was in the films, it had been more sensitive. Seeing him as if sleeping ... at peace.

Lights were beginning to be switched on in the houses as she walked homeward.

Yes, he was at peace. It was a very pleasing last image of him. She would hold it in her mind's eye for a long, long time.

A very long time.

Ainsclough halted the car outside the address on Claremont Road, Kilburn. It revealed itself to be a mid-terraced property in a line of neatly painted late-Victorian four-floored terraced housing, directly across from a cutting in which ran the overground railway line. The address was, not surprisingly to the officers, found to be a multi-occupancy house. Once housing the

44

family for which it was designed, it now had six doorbells beside the front door, not named as such, but labelled Flat 1, Flat 2, etc. Ainsclough pressed them all in turn. 'See what we wake up,' he murmured sourly. When there did not seem to be any reaction from within the house, he banged loudly on the door and shouted, 'Police ... open up!' From inside the house there then came the sound of scurrying feet and then of a toilet being flushed. The officers grinned, and Ainsclough remarked, 'That's this week's supply of dope gone down to the sewers.'

'Aye...' Brunnie stopped smiling and said, 'It also probably means some old lady is going to be robbed of her handbag tonight.'

'No road round it.'

'Nope. Have to give you that,' Brunnie conceded. 'No road round it.'

The door was eventually opened by a timid looking, pale, drawn youth. He had a thin face and unwashed hair. He held the door ajar and peered at Ainsclough and Brunnie through a three inch gap between the door and the frame. 'Police?' He had a thin, rasping voice.

'Yes,' Ainsclough replied, 'but we are not interested in anything you have just flushed down the toilet.'

'You're not?'

'No.'

'So that was a waste of good gear,' Brunnie added.

The youth suddenly looked unwell. He was dressed in a tee shirt and jeans, and was barefoot. 'And we don't even have a search warrant, but we can get one.'

'We want information,' Ainsclough said, 'about a fella who has a room here, Michael Dalkeith.'

'Irish Mickey? He's not in.'

'We know.' Ainsclough spoke quietly. 'In fact, we'd be very, very surprised if you said that he was here. When did you last see him?'

'A week ago ... ten days ... something like that, walked out when the snow was on the ground. He hasn't come back yet.'

'You haven't reported him as a mis per?'

'Mis per?'

'Missing person.'

'No.' The youth shrugged. 'That's Irish Mickey, he goes away for days at a time and he's got family in Palmers Green or someplace, so he told us once ... and he stays out all night earning money.'

'He's on the dole. Unemployed.'

'You try surviving on the dole. You can't do it. Not in London anyway. You got to do

46

a little bobbin' and weavin' ... a little duckin' and divin' if you want to keep your old tin and lead above the wet stuff.'

'Is that right?'

'It's how it is.'

'Are you duckin' and divin'? Is your head above water?'

Again the youth shrugged. 'I don't go stealin', I'm not a crook. I got a job washing up at the Chinese food joint.'

'Washing dishes?'

'They pay cash and I get a meal at the beginning of each shift, keeps me alive.'

'And the DSS don't know about it?'

'Nope ... I mean, do me a favour, the nice thing about those DSS snoopers is that they only snoop during office hours.'

'Is that a fact?'

'So they say ... and I take a different route to work each evening and a different route home. There's a whole hidden army working at night for cash; you need to moonlight. Irish Mickey was like that, he'd be away for a day or two, come back with hard cash in his pocket; more than I could earn but we never asked questions. So he keeps a drum here but his Giro goes to another address. We don't get much post.'

'Which is his room?'

The youth pointed to the window beside

the front door. 'That's his, downstairs front. Nobody wants a front room, too noisy ... got noise from the street and you've got noise from the railway, so the last person in the house gets the downstairs front, the second last gets the upstairs front. Me, I got the back room.'

'So, Mickey Dalkeith was the last lodger to move in?'

'Yes.'

'Which was when?'

'About a year ago. It's a fairly settled drum. I've been here two years, I'm comfortable. There are better, there are worse, but I'm happy. Queen's Park tube and railway station is at the end of the street and it's not too far to walk to work.'

'We need to look inside Mickey's room.'

'Why?'

Ainsclough pushed the door open, and as the youth stumbled backwards, he said, 'Let's just say we're interested and let's just say a warrant won't be needed.' Ainsclough and Brunnie entered the house and instantly fought for breath, the heavy malodorous air within smelling, it seemed, of a combination of damp and kitchen smells, both compounded by a lack of sufficient ventilation.

'Don't you open windows in this house?'

Brunnie complained.

'You get used to it.' The youth sank back against the wall, merging with the gloom.

Ainsclough tried to open the door to Michael Dalkeith's room and found it secured by a barrel lock, but only loosely so. He shoved the door and it opened easily. He turned to the youth. 'Thanks for your help. So sling it, unless you want us to search your room as well.' The youth quickly 'slung it', climbing the stairs hurriedly and silently. The officers stepped into the darkness that was Michael Dalkeith's room.

The body on the bed was that of a young female. Naked. Eyes open, arms and legs raised in rigor. Body fluid had drained from the eye sockets and had solidified at the side of her head. She was Northern European and had short blonde hair. She was thin and wasted in terms of her appearance. She was bruised about the throat.

Ainsclough and Brunnie glanced at each other.

'So what do you think?' Ainsclough reached for his mobile phone. 'Strangled her and then went for a walk in the snow? Murder/suicide ... the alternative being a life stretch?'

'Possibly,' Brunnie murmured. 'Certainly looks that way. We'll need to speak to everyone in the house. I'll round them up.'

Ainsclough nodded. 'I'll ask for assistance...'

Brunnie walked out of the room as Ainsclough requested the attendance of a senior officer, SOCO, pathologist and a vehicle to 'remove persons to custody'. He went up the stairs, which creaked under his weight, and knocked on the bedroom door at the back of the house, opening it before the occupant could ask him to enter. The youth stood in the middle of the floor looking lost and helpless. 'Who else is in the house?' Brunnie demanded.

'Just the women. Front room.'

'What about the top floor?'

'Empty. Three rooms up there but the landlord doesn't let them out. Go and look if you don't believe me.'

'Oh, I will, don't worry. A landlord that doesn't let rooms out...'

'Used for storage. He's got other properties. The upstairs rooms are full of furniture and stuff.'

'I see. Well, get some clothes on and some shoes, you're going for a ride.'

'I'm working this evening.'

'Possibly. Possibly not. Get ready, and go and wait in the kitchen. So, the two women share one room?'

'Yes, but that's their business ... if you see what I mean.'

'So what about the girl, the girl in the front downstairs room?'

'Oh, her?'

'Yes, her.'

'She doesn't really live here ... she stays now and again. Mickey brought her home a few weeks ago. She comes and goes. Didn't know she was in the house to be honest.'

'What do you know about her?'

'Not a lot. Welsh girl ... Gaynor ... she's dead young, teenage runaway.'

'You're right there ... about her being dead young. Now, get some more clothes on and go to the kitchen.'

'Why?'

'Because the house is now a crime scene and we're going to search it.'

'Search...' The youth's face paled even further.

'Why? You got something we might be interested in?'

'Just a bit of blow, sir.'

'Thought you'd flushed it.'

'That was those two women. Me, I took a chance.'

'How much have you got?'

'Just enough for two spliffs, sir.'

'So not supplying?'

51

'Oh ... no ... no, sir.'

'So why are you shaking like a leaf?'

'I'm under a two year suspended sentence ... for possession. So any conviction, even a minor one, will have me in the big house for two years.'

Brunnie paused. 'OK, I'm going to talk to those two women you mentioned. Better flush what you've got, but mind our dogs can detect the slightest, and I mean the slightest, trace ... so for this I want co-operation.'

'Yes, sir ... about what?'

'The murder of the Welsh runaway.'

The youth made a strangled cry, 'Murder! I saw nothing.'

'You'll have seen something ... you'll know something ... so flush it and get down below.'

Brunnie walked along the landing and knocked on the door of the upstairs front room.

Five minutes later the three tenants of the house were mustered in the kitchen, which had newspapers for floor covering and a pile of unwashed plates and pans in the sink. It seemed to be the rule that if you wanted to cook a meal in the house, you first had to wash whatever it was you might need, and upon cooking and eating said meal, you left anything you had used to be washed by the next hungry tenant. The youth gave his name as William 'Billy' Kemp. The larger of the two women, who wore jeans and boots, gave her name as Sonya Clements, and the slighter of the two, who wore an ankle-length dress and heels, gave her name as Josie Pinder. They said they were 'girl-friends'.

'Here's how it works,' Brunnie addressed the three tenants who stood in attentive silence. 'You cooperate with us and we'll cooperate with you. The girl who lived in the front room with Mickey Dalkeith ... she's been murdered.'

The two women looked at each other. Billy Kemp remained expressionless. Brunnie thought their reactions to be genuine. No one displayed any sign of guilt, none overacted in feigned shock or surprise. 'So work with us and we'll work with you.' He paused as he glanced down the hallway and out into the street as a dark-blue police minibus halted at the kerb. 'OK, here's your transport. Non-cooperation from you and we'll turn your rooms over until we find something we can use against you. Give us mucho info and we'll turn a blind eye to little things like a few spliffs. Is that right, Billy?'

'Yes, sir.'

'See, I let Billy flush a few things ... in an act of good faith ... and you ladies flushed something when we knocked on the door; there'll be more to find and we'll find it if we have to. OK, out into the street and into the van.'

The three residents filed out of the building and Brunnie noted that not one could resist a sideways glance into the gloom of the front downstairs room, and then they stepped out of the house and climbed meekly into the police vehicle and were driven away.

Harry Vicary turned into Claremont Road just as the police minibus drew away from the kerb. He drove his car slowly and parked it at the kerb in the space vacated by the police van. Ignoring the members of the public who stood on the pavement, having noticed the activity at the house, he walked into the hallway and, directed by a constable, into the front room of the house. He encountered a dimly lit room and a musty atmosphere. DS Ainsclough and a slightly built man stood in the room. Vicary noticed the corpse lying on the bed. He also noticed the cluttered and untidy nature of the room, and was unable to tell if there had been a struggle; the room, he thought, could best be described as chaotic.

'Dr Rothwell–' Ainsclough indicated the slightly built young man – 'the duty police surgeon.'

'Ah.' Vicary extended his hand. 'DS Vicary.'

'Nice to meet you, sir.' Rothwell shook Vicary's hand warmly. 'Well, I have confirmed life extinct.' He spoke with a distinct West Country accent. 'And I think it is suspicious. Contusions to the neck, open eyes ... petechial haemorrhaging ... but that is for the next box, so to speak.'

'Understood.' Vicary glanced at Ainsclough. 'SOCO? Home Office pathologist?'

'Both requested, sir.'

'Well, no need for me to remain.' Rothwell closed his Gladstone bag. 'I have another call to make. It's going to be one of those nights. No rest for the wicked.' Rothwell stepped lightly out of the room and exited the house.

'Brunnie?' Vicary asked.

'Here, sir.' Brunnie entered the room. 'Just taken a quick sweep of the house – all the attic rooms seem to have been used for storage ... furniture in the main. So, just three other residents, all taken in for questioning. Detailed search has not yet been done.'

'I see.'

55

'The deceased is believed to be called Gaynor Davies, from Wales. One resident said she was a teenage runaway.'

'Teenage?' Vicary glanced at the slight figure. 'She'd pass for eleven or twelve.'

'Yes, sir.' Brunnie spoke softly. 'I know what you mean.'

'She was brought back by Michael Dalkeith and she lived here, coming and going as she pleased when he was away, which was for days at a time.'

'He had a family in Palmers Green, sir,' Ainsclough said. 'Wife and two stepchildren ... but kept the rental on this place ... in which he also lived with the deceased.'

'Sounds like he would have had some explaining to do if he hadn't lain down in the snow. Two addresses, a female in each address, one of whom is now deceased, and deceased in suspicious circumstances.'

There came a knock on the front door. They stopped talking and glanced towards the door of the room as the constable stepped to one side and said, 'In here, sir.'

Moments later the squat figure of John Shaftoe bumbled into the room. He smiled and said, 'Hello, boys.'

'Sir,' Vicary replied.

Shaftoe smiled at Vicary. 'Didn't think I'd see thee again today, Mr Vicary. No rest for the wicked, eh?'

'Funny you should say that,' Vicary said with a wry grin.

'Oh?'

'Nothing ... nothing, sir.' Vicary replied. 'It just struck a private chord ... The deceased ... female ... life was pronounced extinct.'

Ainsclough checked his notepad, 'At seventeen fifty-eight hours, sir.'

'Seventeen fifty-eight,' Vicary repeated.

'I see.' Shaftoe looked at the body. 'You're too young to be a customer of mine, pet, far too young. She doesn't look much older than twelve.'

'We're told she is a teenager, sir.'

'Yes, she could be a finely built thirteen or fourteen, but I'd be surprised if she was much older than that.' He paused. 'Strangulation, it seems.'

'Yes, sir. The police surgeon who has just left said much the same thing.'

'Have you photographed the corpse?'

'Not yet, sir.'

'I see ... so can't be moved yet?'

'No, sir, not overmuch.'

'If you can turn her over, I can take a rectal temperature. It might help determine the time of death, although time of death is an inexact science at best, really no more accurate than sometime between when she

57

was last seen alive and when the corpse was discovered, but the Home Office like thoroughness. So, I'll take a rectal temperature and a room temperature, then, frankly, nothing I can do until I get her to the London Hospital. So I'll do that, undertake the post-mortem tomorrow. Leave you to await the scene of crime officers, and their cameras and fingerprinting kit and whatever.'

'Very good, sir.'

Vicary despatched Ainsclough and Brunnie to New Scotland Yard. They had reports to write and statements to take from Billy Kemp, Sonya Clements and Josie Pinder. He remained at the scene with three constables and a sergeant.

John Shaftoe, who did not drive, was conveyed to the London Hospital by his driver in a small black car. He went to his office and opened a medical file on the as yet unnamed female found deceased, possibly strangled, in the house on Claremont Road, Kilburn. He locked his medical bag in a secure cabinet and then, pulling on a donkey jacket and a flat cap, he left the hospital by an obscure side entrance and walked into the enveloping darkness of London's East End. An observer would have seen a low-skilled manual worker, short and stocky, ambling homeward after a good day's graft, which was exactly the image that John Shaftoe, MD, MRCP, FRCPath, wanted to portray.

He walked by the walls of the buildings, this being a practice he had acquired during his youth in south Yorkshire, where 'hard' men who wanted a fight walked close to the kerb, and feeling disinclined to battle his way through what he always thought to be the oddly ill-named rush hour, he called in at a pub and stood at the bar with his foot on the brass rail, enjoying a pint of IPA. Eventually, as often happened, one of the locals came and stood alongside him. The two men nodded at each other. Shaftoe read the man as being an East End villain and even though, at just 5' 4" tall, Shaftoe was as least cop-like as can be, he still had to be checked out.

'Doing OK, mate?' the East End villain asked with a smile.

'So, so,' Shaftoe replied, avoiding eye contact.

'Not seen you in here before?'

'Not been in here before.' Shaftoe pronounced here as 'ere' and before as 'a-for'.

'North country?' the villain explored, pronouncing north as 'nawf' and country as 'can-ry'.

'Sheffield.'

'Holiday?'

'This time of year?' Shaftoe smiled and allowed himself brief eye contact with his interrogator. He glanced at the TV screen above the bar which showed a cartoon film with the sound blessedly turned off. What sound there was in the pub came from piped music and conversation. It was, observed Shaftoe, already crowded for an early midweek evening. 'No, visiting me sister, she's been taken badly ... but she'll be alright. Just came in for a wander, to have a look at London,' pronouncing have as 'av' and London as 'Lundun'.

'Alright,' the wide-boy replied, pronouncing it as 'or-white'. He then walked back to his mates and said loudly. 'He's alright, down from the north,' and then added pointedly, 'He won't be staying long.' And John Shaftoe, taking the hint, finished his drink and left the pub. Sometimes it was like that. He felt he had to avoid becoming a regular in one particular pub near the London Hospital, because if he did so, his occupation would eventually be discovered and he would no longer be allowed to blend with the other patrons, which was all he wanted to do. He and his wife sometimes just needed to be 'working class'. So it was that sometimes he walked into a welcoming pub and sometimes he stumbled into a thieves' den, which was hostile to anyone they did not know. That night he had clearly entered the latter type of pub. He would take note and avoid it in future.

By the time he left the bar of the not so jolly Jolly Boatman, dark had fallen and the rush hour, while still on, had also begun to ease. He took the Metropolitan line from Whitechapel tube station to King's Cross, and then took an overground train bound for Welwyn. He left the train at Brookmans Park, exited the station via the footbridge and, with his hands thrust into the pockets of his donkey jacket, looking like a coal miner returning home from a shift at the pit, he walked into the leafy suburbs and up Brookmans Lane, which was softly illuminated by street lamps. Large, fully detached houses were situated on either side of the road, many with U-shaped driveways; thus the homeowners avoided having to reverse their cars into the lane. The houses all had generous back gardens, and those to his left backed on to the golf course and thereby afforded even more open space to survey when standing at the rear windows of said houses. He felt himself thinking, aren't we smug, as he walked. But the smug occupants of these houses were also his neighbours, because although he and his wife liked to drink in working-class pubs 'to touch base', they were both disinclined to live on a sink estate and had bought what property they could manage to afford on his salary as a learned Home Office pathologist, and so, working class or not, they had eventually fetched up in 'smug, self-satisfied' Brookmans Park, Hertfordshire.

He turned right into one such large house, which had all the front room lights turned on, with a U-shaped drive – though the car by the door was only a modest Volkswagen – and unlocked the front door. He peeled off his jacket as Linda Shaftoe, tall and slender, and, he always thought, holding back the years with admirable success, greeted him warmly. 'Good day, pet?' She took his jacket from him as he sat on the bench beside the front door and began to tug at his shoelaces.

'Busy,' he said, easing his right foot out of a tightly fitting shoe, 'busy enough to make me glad to be home.'

'Well ... good, hot stew in the pot for you.'

'Champion, pet.' He eased the other shoe off his foot and reached for his slippers. 'Champion.'

★ ★ ★

Harry Vicary surveyed the room. It was, he felt, the room of a lowlife murderer; there was a tangible cheapness of life about the four walls and the space within which reached him, deeply so. He sensed that here in this room, humanity had little value. The contents, too, were cheap, inexpensive; they seemed to have a careworn, overused, second-hand quality about them. The cluttered room also had a sense of age, as though the contents had been allowed to accumulate over time. Snapping on a pair of latex gloves he began gingerly to open the drawers of the dressing table, ensuring that the police constable then present was watching him closely as he did so. He needed a witness for anything he might find, and also a witness that he did not unlawfully remove anything. He found little of apparent interest: some loose change, a rent book in the name of one Jennifer Reeves, which seemed to be there because no one had thrown it out – the last rent collection entered being some ten years previously. Yet, the clutter in the room suggested to him a longer-term tenant than Michael Dalkeith, who had reportedly moved into the room some twelve months previously. The seemingly long-established musty smell also seemed to speak of a long-term tenant. The

63

owner of the property, as given on the dated rent book, was WLM Rents of Kilburn, with an address in Fernhead Road.

'Fernhead Road?' Vicary turned to the constable.

'Just round the corner, sir,' the young, serious-minded constable replied. 'It's the main road round here.'

'Ah ... thanks. One to be visited tomorrow.'

'Sir?'

'Oh, just muttering to myself. The landlord will be someone to visit; see what he can tell us about his tenants.'

'Yes, sir.'

'Notice anything about the room, constable?'

'Messy, sir.'

'Yes ... too messy for someone who has just moved in...'

'Now you mention it, sir. Confess I hadn't read that.'

'These things you will learn, these observations you will be taught to make.'

'Yes, sir.'

'And a deceased female also.'

'So I believe, sir, but I came just now, sir, just as the body was being removed.'

'Yes, I know ... but no female clothing. I haven't looked in all the drawers yet, but I'd still expect to see a woman's coat or pair of shoes ... something like that.'

'Yes ... or a handbag, sir.'

'Yes ... good observation, no handbag either. Runaways are unlikely to have a handbag but only unlikely ... so it's a good observation. The door was locked ... easily forced but still locked; no one had come in and rifled the room. Sorry, just musing again.'

'Yes, sir.'

'He brings the girl in, brings her from somewhere ... strangles her, takes all her clothing and her handbag, and heaven only knows what else ... and then goes for a walk on Hampstead Heath in a blizzard ... and does so ill-dressed for the weather conditions on that day or night, or whenever, and then lies down in the snow to sleep his final sleep right on top of a corpse that was already there, and had been for a number of years.'

'You mean like he knew it was there, sir, like he was leading us there, sir? Telling us about the corpse?'

Vicary looked at the constable and did so with widening eyes and a slackening jaw.

TWO

WLM Rents occupied the ground floor of a house on Fernhead Road, Kilburn. Vicary had never before set foot in Fernhead Road. It was a narrow road, he found, probably wide enough to accommodate vehicular traffic in the late nineteenth century, when the tall, elegant terrace houses which stood on either side of the tree-lined road were built, but now, in twenty-first-century Britain, it would, Vicary thought, be a bottleneck during the rush hour. He walked into the office of WLM Rents and was met by a bright, airy interior, smelling of air freshener, with large colour photographs of London landmarks – Trafalgar Square, the Tower, Westminster Bridge – attached to the walls. A water dispenser, filled with mineral water, stood in the corner by the door. Comfortable looking upholstered chairs lined one wall and in front of them were two coffee tables standing end to end, upon which lay copies of *London Life*, *Time Out* and other magazines about living in London and the Home Counties. Upon Vicary and Brunnie entering the premises, a young man, dressed in a suit and tie, stood smartly, smiled and said, 'Good morning, gentlemen. How can I help you?'

'Police.' Vicary showed his ID.

'Oh.' The man, J.J. Dunwoodie by the nameplate on his desk, paled. 'No bother, I hope?'

'Plenty.' Vicary smiled. 'Always, always, always plenty of bother ... no shortage of bother at all, keeps us in gainful employment, but we are here only to seek a little information.'

'Of course.' Dunwoodie indicated two easy chairs with wooden arms that stood in front of his desk. The officers took a seat, and only when they were seated did the young Dunwoodie also sit. He was, thought Vicary, a young man who seemed conscientious and took his job very seriously, although working for a private landlord would, he mused, offer limited potential for advancement and would not have the generous conditions of the service enjoyed by public or civil servants. He said to himself, 'You can do better than this, young Dunwoodie. Much, much better,' but he said aloud, 'We understand that WLM

Rents owns a property near here, specifically on Claremont Road, by the railway, particularly number 123; can't forget that house number. Very convenient.'

'Oh, yes.'

'You seem to know it?' Vicary noticed Brunnie take his notepad from his coat pocket and a pen from the inside pocket of his sports jacket.

'Yes, I do, I know it well, but it is not typical of WLM Rents.'

'Oh?'

'Oh, not at all, WLM is more upmarket than 123. We rent to young, professional people. Number 123 is one of our ancillary properties.'

'Ancillary properties?'

'It will be developed soon, when Mr William is ready. It has been an ancillary property for a year or two.'

'And you have permission from the local authority to use it as business premises?'

'Yes, all legal and proper. It was derelict and Mr William negotiated the change on the deeds as part of the condition of undertaking its development. It was a real eyesore; in fact an oak tree was growing up from the basement. So the local authority was pleased when someone was prepared to take on the renovation. It gave Mr William a bit of leverage you might say, to negotiate the change to the deeds.'

'I see.'

'So ... 123 is awaiting development, then we'll rent it to the young professionals. Kilburn is very convenient for the City so we have a lot of bankers and stockbrokers on our books. I mean, direct tube to central London, just one change to reach the Square Mile; our tenants are between university and their first mortgage. That's how Mr William made his fortune.'

'Oh?'

'Yes. He's a stockbroker. He made a killing about twenty years ago and he used his money to buy up as much of Kilburn as he could. He saw the potential of the area. He knew it would be gentrified and he was right, money came in from rents and he bought more houses, and he now has over one hundred properties ... all in Kilburn. He is known as the King of Kilburn.'

'How interesting.'

'Yes. He has done well.' Dunwoodie beamed.

'So tell us about the house on Claremont Road?'

'Yes ... well, run down ... can't rent it as it is, not to the sort of person we want to deal with. So it's used for storing furniture, but we also use it as a grace and favour residence for people who do the occasional odd job for the company.'

'Grace and favour?'

'Yes, it's hardly a St James's Palace sort of grace and favour residence but it keeps the squatters out. The people in the ancillary properties don't pay rent but Mr William asks them for favours from time to time.'

'And if they say "no" they'll be in the street?'

Dunwoodie looked rather uncomfortable. 'Well...' he stammered.

'How many such properties does he have?'

'About ten ancillaries ... mostly young women are in them, some young men.'

Vicary and Brunnie glanced at each other. Vicary then looked back at Dunwoodie. 'So where do we find Mr William?'

'At home ... sometimes he calls in here to water the plants.'

'The plants?'

'Yes, he's quite green-fingered.' Dunwoodie pointed to a line of potted plants which stood on a series of red filing cabinets. 'He likes to keep the plants watered. It gets hot and dry in here. I could do it, the watering can is there, but he likes to do it. But mostly he works at home.'

'What is his home address?'

'His main home is in Virginia Water.'

'It would be,' Brunnie growled. 'What's the address?'

'I can phone him to ask him if I can give you his number.'

'Address!'

'I don't know it, just his phone number. But I am not supposed to give it to anyone; he's very clear on that point.'

'We're not anybody,' Vicary snarled. 'The number!'

'Really, I am under strict instructions—'

'You could be arrested and charged with obstruction. This is a murder enquiry.'

'Murder!' Dunwoodie gasped.

'Yes. Murder. With a capital "M".'

J.J. Dunwoodie reached for the file index on his desk and began to thumb through it. 'Old fashioned, I know, but so what, it works. Ah ... here it is, Mr William Pilcher.' He read out Pilcher's phone number and Brunnie wrote it in his notebook. 'I'll have to phone Mr William and let him know that you called and demanded his phone number.'

'Do that,' Vicary replied. 'And tell him to expect us very soon.'

'Soon?'

'As in just how long it will take us to drive from here to Virginia Water,' Brunnie explained. 'That sort of soon. Have a good day.'

John Shaftoe pulled down the microphone until it was level with his mouth and cast a despairing eye at the trembling and twitching Billy Button, who looked at the corpse with undisguised fear.

'You know, Billy,' Shaftoe leaned on the stainless steel table, resting his fleshy hands on the raised lip, 'you could do worse than put it all into context for yourself.'

'Sir? What do you mean, sir?'

'Well ... tell me ... how old are you now?'

'Me, sir, I'm fifty-seven, sir.'

'Fifty-seven?'

'Yes, sir, last July.'

'Alright.'

'So just three years short of your three score ... just thirteen years short of your three score and ten...'

'Suppose so, sir.'

'And you're still going strong.'

'Suppose that too, sir.'

'OK. Well, look at this fella here on the table.' Shaftoe nodded to the corpse of Michael Dalkeith which lay face up on the table with a starched white towel draped over the genitalia. 'How old do you think he is – or was – when he died?'

Button shrugged. 'Forty, sir?'

'Probably younger than that, probably a lot younger. I saw the conditions he lived in: one room in a shared house in Kilburn across the street from the railway line. So do you want to swap places with him? Would you want his living conditions rather than your own?'

'No, sir.'

'No, sir ... right, sir, you've already lived longer than he has lived ... lucky you. And you've a wife and a home to go back to each evening. He was born when you were already alive and you're still alive now that he is no more. What have you ... you and me both ... what have we got to complain of?'

'Well ... since you put it like that, sir...'

'Nothing is the answer. Nothing.'

'Yes, sir.'

'And the next PM we will be doing today, just a lassie, barely in her teens. I've seen her corpse ... wasted wee soul; she was brought in last night – almost like a skeleton covered in parchment. So context, Billy ... context.'

'Yes, sir.'

'And if it's being cut open after you are dead that scares you?'

'Yes, sir ... those shiny instruments.'

'I've told you before; the chances are it won't happen.'

'Yes, sir.'

'Right.' Shaftoe reached for the microphone at the end of the anglepoise arm and switched it on. 'The corpse is that of a well-nourished adult of the male sex who has been positively identified as one Michael Dalkeith of Palmers Green, who had also been resident in Kilburn. All details are with the police. The interested police officer is Detective Inspector Harry Vicary of the Murder and Serious Crime Squad of New Scotland Yard.' Shaftoe paused. 'There are no evident injuries. The deceased was found in an exposed place when the recent snow thawed, giving the clear indication that he had succumbed to hypothermia.' He took a scalpel, and placing it at the throat of the deceased, drew it downwards over the chest to the stomach and then divided the incision to the left and the right, thus forming an inverted 'Y' on the man's torso. 'I am performing a standard midline incision,' he said calmly for the benefit of the tape. Shaftoe peeled the skin back, exposing the internal organs. 'Better take a deep breath, Billy,' Shaftoe said as he pressed the tip of the scalpel into the stomach. He also took a deep breath and turned his head away as the stomach gasses hissed upon their release. He waved his hand in the air and took a step

74

backwards. 'I've smelled worse,' he said, smiling, 'a lot worse.'

'Yes, sir.'

'Actually, that is not bad.' Shaftoe peered into the stomach, 'Oh, one hungry boy. He hadn't eaten anything for ... for probably forty-eight hours before he died, certainly twenty-four ... but he is so healthy, so well-nourished, yet the empty stomach would have made it even more difficult for him to withstand the cold. That is quite strange.'

Shaftoe took an electrically powered circular saw and cut down the centre of the rib-cage, thus separating the ribs. 'The heart appears healthy.' Using the scalpel, he sep-arated the organ from the body and placed it on a set of scales. 'Heart is age/ weight proportional. I'll dissect it later but I am sure it was healthy.' Shaftoe took the circular saw and cut round the circumference of the skull, just above the ears, and then lifted the top of the skull away. It separated with a loud sucking sound. 'Similarly,' Shaftoe said for the benefit of the microphone, 'the brain appears healthy. Nice thick skull also ... lucky man. You know, Billy, I once did a PM on a young lad, just eight years old, who died of a fractured skull which led to brain damage. The story was that his dad had clipped him round the ear for being cheeky to his mum … and succeeded in killing him. Turned out that the poor lad had an egg-shell skull, so called, no thicker than a single sheet of newspaper. I told the inquest that any minor blow to the head could – in fact, would – have been fatal. If he played soccer and had headed the ball, he would then have lost his life. The poor lad was just a fatal accident waiting to happen. Any rough and tumble with his mates, any accidental knock to the head would have killed him. The coroner recorded a verdict of acciden-tal death, which was a fair verdict but the boy's father was beside himself with grief and guilt. So that's something else to mea-sure your life against, Billy. Context … con-text.'

'Yes, sir.'

Shaftoe took the brain and weighed it. 'The brain is of normal weight for the age of the deceased.' He placed the brain on the working surface and, taking a knife, he sliced it thinly. 'All healthy,' he said, 'no stroke victim he. I will send a blood sample for a toxicology examination, but in the absence of poison, I will record a finding of death due to hypothermia, compounded by the empty stomach and insufficient clothing at the time of death. The empty stomach is puzzling though, very puzzling given his overall well-nourished state. This PM might not yet be complete. See what the toxicology test reveals, if anything.'

Hollow Hill, Virginia Water, Surrey. Large houses, large in any man's language, were set back from the road, each house separated from the neighbouring property by small stands of woodland; large front gardens, larger back gardens, which gave way to an area of woodland. Vicary at the wheel, and Brunnie beside him in the passenger seat, sat in silence, though both men thought the same: here be money. Big money.

The house owned by the proprietor of WLM Rents sat well, it seemed to Vicary, with its neighbours. It was not significantly larger, nor markedly smaller than the other houses on the road. It blended, Vicary conceded, and did so neatly – painted in a soft green about the window frames and doors, faded brickwork under a brown tiled roof, with a double garage to the right-hand side. The broad driveway expanded into a wide courtyard in front of the house. To the left of the drive was a raised rockery of about ten feet high, which prevented any very occasional foot passenger passing along the pavement from looking into the house. The front door was enclosed within a solid wooden porch, with windows in the door and at either side. A small window at ground level to the left of the porch betrayed the existence of a cellar. Vicary turned into the driveway and halted the car beside the royal-blue Range Rover which was parked close to the door. 'Dare say the Rolls-Royce is in the garage,' he remarked as he switched off the car's ignition.

'Dare say it is—' Brunnie smiled as he unclipped his seat belt – 'next to the Bentley. How much do you think it's worth?'

'I wouldn't like to guess.' Vicary glanced at the house. 'Well out of our league, that's for sure.' The house was clearly an inter-war building, modern in many respects, but built when houses were still being built to last. His father-in-law's warning of 'Don't even look at anything built after 1939' had proved to be good advice for him and his wife.

Vicary and Brunnie left the car and walked up to the porch, but the door of the house opened before Vicary could press the doorbell. The man stepped forward and opened the porch door. He had a hard, humourless looking face, clean-shaven, cold blue eyes, close-cropped hair. He wore cream-coloured cavalry twill trousers and a white shirt, over which was a pale-blue woollen pullover. His feet were encased in highly polished brown shoes. The only jewellery was a Rolex on his left wrist.

'You'll be the police,' he said. He spoke with a hard voice, almost, Vicary thought, a rasping sound, and both he and Brunnie recognized the type: a career criminal.

'Yes, sir.' Vicary showed his ID. Brunnie did the same. 'I'm DI Vicary. This is DC Brunnie. Scotland Yard.'

'Scotland Yard? It must be serious ... must be important. You'd better come in. My man only told me the police were calling to see me. He didn't mention Scotland Yard.'

The officers entered a wide entrance hall, thickly carpeted, with stained and polished panelling on the walls, and a wide staircase angling up to the first floor. From the entrance hall they were shown into a room just to the right of the front door, which was clearly used to entertain official visitors. Evidently only guests were allowed to enter the inner areas of the house. Officials, and especially police officers, were kept by the door. The room itself was spartan in the extreme, with no floor covering, though the floorboards had been sanded and varnished, and four inexpensive, office-style easy chairs stood round a glass-topped coffee table.

Though the room was still larger, Brunnie guessed, than the living room of his flat in Walthamstow, E17. The wallcovering was of green embossed wallpaper, which seemed to Vicary to be of the same vintage as the house and, when needed, the illumination would come from a single light bulb, which hung from the ceiling and was enveloped in a yellow, bowl-like glass shade dating from the 1930s. The room seemed to Vicary to be deliberately arranged to be uncomfortable, cold, unwelcoming and very hostile, and it had, he thought, a hard cell-like quality, with nothing, nothing at all such as a print on the wall or a plant in a pot, to offer any form of softening.

'Do take a seat, please.' The man spoke in a perfunctory manner. The words kept to the script, but the tone of voice was as cold and as hard as the room. Vicary, Brunnie and the householder sat down; Vicary and Brunnie side by side, the man opposite them, with the coffee table separating him and the officers. 'So,' he said, 'how can I help you, gentlemen?'

'You are?'

'William Pilcher.'

'You own WLM Rents?'

'Yes, WLM of course being derived from my given name.'

'I see.'

'And yes, WLM Rents is my little portfolio.' He smiled. 'The stock market was ... useful to me once.'

'So we understand from Mr Dunwoodie.'

'J.J. Yes, he's a good little beaver to have working for me. So, how can I help you?'

'We are particularly interested in one of your properties in Kilburn.'

'They are all in Kilburn. I began buying up Kilburn when I realized the properties were undervalued and the area was set for gentrification. Close enough to fall into the spill of the beam from Hampstead and Golders Green.'

'The property on Claremont Road, 123 Claremont Road; Mr Dunwoodie described it as an ancillary property.'

'Yes, awaiting development.'

'Mr Dunwoodie described it as a "grace and favour" house.'

'He did?'

'Yes, he did.'

'He does tend to be ... don't know the word ... but yes, I let people live there and they work for me, low-grade gofers really. They pay no rent, but if I need a favour, they oblige.'

'So Mr Dunwoodie explained.'

'Did he?' A menacing growl entered

Pilcher's voice to the extent that Vicary felt a sudden chill of fear for the welfare of J.J. Dunwoodie. Working for Pilcher evidently did not mean you enjoyed the man's protection.

'We are making enquiries into a man called Michael Dalkeith.'

'Irish Mickey? What about him?'

'He is deceased.'

'Oh, I'm sorry to hear that. I knew he had gone, seemed that he did a moonlight, but he didn't owe me any money so I wasn't too upset.'

'So how did you know him? In what capacity did you know him?'

Pilcher shrugged in an uninterested way. Vicary thought that he did not seem at all concerned about the death of Michael 'Irish Mickey' Dalkeith. 'He was an odd-job man. He did a little work now and then. He was no craftsman, just the old donkey jobs.'

'Donkey jobs?'

'Fetching and carrying, tidying up, making the tea for the working crew ... that number.'

'You paid him in cash?'

'Yes, he preferred it that way.'

'So he could claim dole money?'

'Yes, the old, black economy number.' Pilcher paused. 'Mind you, it was peanuts, his pay really was his rent-free accommodation, and that was worth a few hundred pounds a week.'

'How long did he live at Claremont Road?'

'On and off for a good few months, possibly about a year. He took up with a woman in North London somewhere and then returned – kept a girl in the room so I believe. Really it was J.J. that handled it; I had more important issues to work on.'

'Alright, we'll go back and have another chat with Dunwoodie, because you see there is a little more to it...'

'Oh?'

'Yes, the girl you mentioned...'

'Yes?'

'Well, she is also deceased.'

'Oh, my, what has been going on at that house?'

'That's what we want to know; also the other tenants are in custody and won't be going anywhere soon. So, what do you know of the girl?'

'Nothing about her. I heard that she was living with him but I have no interest in employees' private lives. The purpose of the people in the ancillary properties is to keep the squatters out and do some occasional unskilled work. Like I said, I am a businessman and I am focused on other issues. If that is all...'

Vicary and Brunnie stood. 'Yes, that is all ... for now.'

'For now?' Pilcher also stood.

'We never know what might develop, so yes, "for now".' Vicary smiled and walked to the door. He then turned and said, 'Oh, just one thing...'

'Yes?'

'When "Irish Mickey" Dalkeith died, face down in the snow on Hampstead Heath, he had no food in his stomach, yet the pathologist said he was well-nourished.'

'So?'

'So, a well-nourished man with no food in his stomach is a puzzle.'

'It is?'

'It suggests that he had been starved of food for a day or two before he died.'

'Dare say it might suggest that.'

'Well, it might mean something, it might not. Very early days yet and we're in no hurry, but we are very dogged, eh, DC Brunnie?'

'We are that, sir.' Brunnie smiled at Pilcher. 'Just as dogged as dogged can be. We don't give up easily.'

'But you know, he did us a favour,' Vicary continued.

'Oh?' Pilcher seemed attentive, more so than hitherto, thought Vicary.

'Yes, you know, he fell down right on top of a shallow grave. Might just be a coincidence, but as one of our constables said, it might also be that he was leading us there, right to the grave ... a young adult female, quite short, about five feet tall, been there a few years ... ten to fifteen years buried, something like that.'

Pilcher paled. His brow furrowed.

'You don't know anything about that?'

'No!' His reply was aggressive, defensive.

'We'll find out who she was soon enough, and all roads will lead to Rome. If there is a connection between the late "Irish Mickey" Dalkeith and the deceased woman who lay concealed under his dead body, we'll find out. Well, we'll say good day, Mr Pilcher. Thank you for your time.'

Driving back to central London, Vicary asked Brunnie what he thought of Pilcher.

'A nasty.' Brunnie glanced to his left as the car slid by the wealth of north-west Surrey, 'too hard to be a stockbroker, like Durham E-wing hard; too ready to get rid of us and too frightened when you mentioned the fact that Dalkeith had died as if leading us to the shallow grave. Frankly, it would not surprise me one little bit if Pilcher was an alias and that he is well known to us under a different handle.'

'Yes.' Vicary smiled but kept looking straight ahead. 'My feelings exactly. We need to find out just who he is – pick that up, will you?'

'Yes, boss, I'll get right on it. My curiosity is well aroused, very well up.'

For the second time that day John Shaftoe considered a corpse which lay upon the stainless steel dissecting table in the pathology laboratory of the London Hospital, although, on the second occasion, he had no need to adjust the height of the microphone which was attached to the anglepoise arm above the table. 'Did you have a good lunch, Billy?' He grinned at his nervous assistant, who he thought was looking more than usually pale and unwell.

'It was OK, sir. Usual hospital canteen food but it filled the gap.'

'Good. So, two in one day, not bad ... once did four in one day. I needed my sleep at the end of that day, I can tell you.'

'Yes, sir,' Button whimpered.

'Well ... let's press on.' Shaftoe spoke clearly for the benefit of the microphone. 'The deceased is a frail-looking, undernourished person of the female sex. She is of

86

Northern European or Caucasian racial extraction. Her age is as yet to be determined, but she is young and post-pubescent, and probably in her early teenage years.' He paused. 'Immediately obvious is the extensive bruising to the neck, which is indicative of strangulation. I also note ligature marks to her wrists.' He pulled up the eyelids, one at a time. 'Petechial haemorrhaging is noted, which further indicates that she was strangled. Care to look?' Shaftoe turned to Ainsclough who was observing the post-mortem for the police.

'Yes, sir.' Ainsclough, clad from head to toe in the requisite green paper coveralls, stepped from the side of the theatre to the dissecting table and stood beside, and slightly behind, Shaftoe.

'Little black dots in the whites of the eyes ... see? Blood spots, sometimes, if not black, they have a reddish hue, always a good indication of strangulation or asphyxiation, but we have to be careful not to jump to conclusions because such can also occur naturally, in the event of a brain haemorrhage, for instance, so this, in itself, is not conclusive proof of murder.'

'I see, sir.'

'But taken together, with the bruising to the neck, I think I am on safe ground to state, unless I find anything to the contrary, that this young girl was murdered by manual strangulation, as opposed to being strangled by use of a ligature.'

'So murder, in that case, sir?'

'Yes. Murder most foul.'

'Thank you, sir.' Ainsclough retreated to the wall of the laboratory where he once again stood in deferential silence.

'So the deceased, who regrettably had a short life, was also short in life in terms of her stature. Can you pass the tape measure, please, Billy?'

Billy Button picked up a yellow retractable metal tape-measure from the bench close to the dissecting table and handed it to Shaftoe, who extended the tape from the head to the balls of the feet of the corpse. 'Four feet ten inches tall or one hundred and forty-seven centimetres in her cotton socks, poor thing. God rest her.' Shaftoe took a metal file and scraped under the fingernails of the deceased, and deposited the detritus thereunder into a self-sealing cellophane sachet. 'She might have clawed at her attacker's face and captured his ... or her ... DNA. Might ... might, but the ligature marks on her wrists indicate that she was restrained peri-mortem, so we'll have to wait and see what forensics can tell us. How old do you think she is, Billy?'

Button shrugged. 'Not old, sir.' Button looked at the thin, wasted frame, the ribs, the thin waist, the painfully thin legs which protruded under the starched white towel that had been placed over her middle, the tiny feet. 'I see what you mean about being fortunate, sir.'

'Yes, it's all a matter of context, Billy, all a matter of context.'

'Yes, sir.'

'So we crack on, we continue. I will avoid damaging the face; she still has to be identified. Any ideas yet, Mr Ainsclough?'

'None as yet, sir. We're trawling through the missing persons reports, but she may be from outside London, as many young people are. If that is the situation here, she will only be registered as a mis per locally, that is local to her home.'

'I see. Well, her hands are undamaged. I'll cut them off and send them to the forensic laboratory together with her nail scrapings. They can lift her fingerprints. She might have a record. She might be known to you.'

'Thank you, sir.'

'So, now we'll see what she had for her last meal ... but, flat tummy, wasted, drawn looks, indicate little intestinal gas, which further indicates a recent time of death. I anticipate an empty stomach, she is close to anorexic.'

Shaftoe took a scalpel and drew it across the stomach. Little gas escaped. He opened up the incision and peered into the stomach cavity. 'Yes, as I suspected. No food at all.' Shaftoe took a length of stainless steel and worked it into the mouth and prised the mouth open causing the jaw to give with a soft, cracking sound. 'Rigor is established,' he announced, 'thus placing the time of death between twenty-four and forty-eight hours ago but that is a very inexact science, as you know.'

'Understood, sir.'

'Ah ... she is British, distinctly UK dentistry, and work was done quite recently, so dental records will be able to confirm any ID if her fingerprints are not on file, or if a relative can't identify her.'

'Yes, sir,' Ainsclough replied, raising his voice to enable it to carry across the laboratory.

'She didn't leave you a message, no notes under the tongue or between her teeth and gums. I'll check the other body cavities and send a blood sample for analysis, but it's looking clearly like a case of strangulation after a period of being restrained. So I assume my report will be for the attention of Mr Vicary?'

'Yes, please, sir.'

Frank Brunnie sat at his desk and read the 'no trace' result from his enquiry.

'That,' he murmured, 'that I do not believe.'

'You sound disappointed.' Penny Yewdall glanced up from her desk which faced Brunnie's. 'Something amiss?'

'What isn't amiss? The whole wretched planet is amiss in one way or another.' Brunnie leaned back and put his feet on his desktop.

'If Harry Vicary catches you sitting like that you're in the soup. You know what recent promotees are like ... new brooms sweeping clean; out to make a name for himself.'

'Yes, he had a narrow escape. He's consolidating now.'

'So I heard. Drink, wasn't it?'

'Drink it was. He was given six months to get his act together, which he not only did, but he also did very well in the Jim Coventry murder.'

'That's the one in which Archie Dew was shot?'

'Yes. Harry did well in that case. So, he

sobered up, impressed their Lordships, got promoted, and he's back on track, but he's out right now ... so...' Brunnie let his feet remain on the desktop. 'But this guy–' Brunnie tapped the computer printout – '"no trace", "not known" ... no way, he's a nasty. He smelled nasty, he looked nasty and I tell you, did he look alarmed when we told him that the guy Irish Mickey Dalkeith had gone to sleep in the snow right over the shallow grave of a woman ... or did he look alarmed? Guess which.'

'I should guess ... er ... alarmed.' Yewdall put her pen down and leaned back in her chair. 'What does the Land Registry say?'

'Same. The house in Virginia Water is registered in the name of one William Pilcher.'

'You need a DNA sample or some item with his fingerprints on it.'

Brunnie grinned. 'For that I will take my feet off the desk for Mr Vicary.'

'You see, pretty girls do have their uses,' Yewdall said with a smile.

'So I am discovering. Fancy a trip out to sunny Kilburn?'

'Not particularly,' Yewdall replied. 'It will take much to drag me to sunny Kilburn, not my favourite part of the Great Wen ... but ... but...'

'But?'

'But anything to get away from this wretched paperwork. I know the value of it, but if I wanted to work in an office I'd have been a secretary or a bank clerk. So, let's go.' She stood and reached for her coat. Brunnie did likewise.

Thirty minutes later, Brunnie and Yewdall entered the premises of WLM Rents on Fernhead Road, W9, and were greeted by J.J. Dunwoodie snapping to attention with his eager to please attitude. Brunnie suddenly felt afraid for the safety of Dunwoodie, having just met his employer. He seemed to Brunnie to be akin to a lamb protecting a tiger.

'Your boss?' Brunnie said, shortly, abruptly.

'Mr William?'

'Yes, we need something he has touched.'

'Oh.' Dunwoodie paled. 'I don't know if I could ... if I should.'

'Why?' Yewdall smiled. 'He couldn't have anything to hide; he's a very respectable, hard-working, clean-living businessman, a veritable pillar of the community.'

'Yes...' Dunwoodie stammered, 'he is ... but.'

'But what? When did he last come here, to this office?' Brunnie pressed.

'Today's ... about two, three days ago. Three days ago in the afternoon, late afternoon.'

'Where did he go?'

'He left to visit a property and then he was returning home.'

'No ... no ... where in here? Where in this office did he go?'

'Well, he went into the back office.' Dunwoodie indicated the door behind to the left of him. 'He keeps that door locked; even I can't go inside there. I don't know what's in there.'

'Even you?'

'Well, I mean that I am the office manager and I can't go in that room. All I need to access are the files kept in the cabinets. Everything I need is in those cabinets.'

'I see, so where else did he walk?'

'Nowhere ... just into the back office, watered the plants, then left to view the property Mr William hopes to acquire.'

'He watered the plants?'

'Yes.' Dunwoodie pointed to a row of six money plants that stood on top of the filing cabinets in terracotta pots.

Brunnie noticed a small, red plastic watering can at the end of the row of money plants. 'Did he use that watering can?'

'Yes ... yes, he did.'

Brunnie walked across the hard-wearing felt carpeting and picked the watering can up by the spout. He took a large plastic bag from the inside of his coat and placed the can within it. 'This will do nicely.' He smiled.

'Can you do that?' Dunwoodie spluttered.

'With your permission,' Yewdall said, also smiling.

'Well, I don't ... I mean...'

'Thanks.' Brunnie turned toward the door. 'We'll return it.'

'Did you buy it locally?' Yewdall asked.

'Yes, the hardware shop, five minutes' walk from here.'

'So go and buy another one, an identical one, then no one will ever know, will they?'

'I will have to tell Mr William,' Dunwoodie squeaked.

'No,' Brunnie turned back and faced Dunwoodie, holding eye contact with him. 'No. No. No. For your own sake ... no.'

'For my own sake?' Dunwoodie's face paled.

'Yes, for your own sake.' Brunnie remained stone-faced. 'Lock up the office and go and buy a watering can from the hardware shop. A watering can identical to this one, and return and place it on top of the filing cabinets.'

'Simple as that,' Yewdall added.

'You know, fella,' Brunnie continued, 'I don't know what you think of your boss, but I can tell you that it won't be the same as what I think about him. So go and buy another watering can and mention our little and very brief visit to no one.'

'No one,' Yewdall added, 'no one.'

In the car, driving southwards in slow moving traffic, Yewdall glanced to her left at the residential houses and occasional shop. 'Any more stunts like that,' she said, 'and you'll have us both put against a wall and shot.'

Brunnie grinned. 'You put the idea in my head, but at least we're going to find out who Pilcher really is, and Dunwoodie will be safe if he buys another watering can and keeps his mouth shut.'

Yewdall turned to him. 'If,' she said coldly, 'if, it's a big if ... a very big if.'

Vicary smiled. It was serious. Very serious, but he managed to smile. In the margin of the report on Michael 'Irish Mickey' Dalkeith's blood toxicity, which spoke of milligrams per millilitre of alcohol being present, John Shaftoe had clearly anticipated Vicary's bewilderment and had written in a neat hand, 'sufficient to knock out a horse'.

Vicary said 'Thank you' aloud and laid the toxicity report to one side, and picked up the post-mortem report, also submitted by John Shaftoe, in respect of the shallowly buried, skeletonized corpse which was found beneath Michael Dalkeith's frozen body. The post-mortem findings had been compared to information on missing persons and Vicary saw that, worryingly, quite a few women of about five feet tall in height had been reported missing, and were still missing, in the Greater London area within the last fifteen years. The vast majority, however, were very young – teenagers or early twenties – but one, just one missing person's report stood out as being the most promising potential match to the post-mortem findings. Rosemary Halkier was thirty-five years old when she was reported missing some ten years earlier. The mother of two children, she had been reported as a missing person by her father with whom she was living at the time in Albert Road, Leyton, which was, as if fate was helpfully intervening, very close to Vicary's route home. If he left the tube train just one stop earlier than usual, he could very easily call in at the Halkier household, make a brief enquiry and then walk home from there in less than fifteen minutes. Vicary glanced out of his office window. He noted the sky to be low and grey but, thankfully, it was not raining, and as such it made a stroll from Leyton to Leytonstone on a dry winter's evening seem very inviting. Very inviting indeed. He stood and worked himself into his overcoat and screwed his fedora hat on to his head. He signed himself 'Out – not coming back', and walked out of the Murder and Serious Crime Unit. He took the lift to the ground floor and exited New Scotland Yard by the main entrance in front of the triangular sign which read, 'Working for a safer London'. He took the District Line to Mile End and there changed on to the Central Line and, as he had planned, left the tube at Leyton.

Albert Road revealed itself to be a residential street lined with solid Victorian terraced housing, but was interspersed with post-Second World War development on the southern side, which, as very frequently in London and other cities in the UK, indicated where bombs had fallen during the Blitz. The Halkier household was, like the houses around it, a clear survivor of Nazi bombs: brick built, white-painted around the front bay window, and a black-gloss-painted door with a brass knocker. A small front garden of just four feet separated the house from the pavement. Vicary pushed open the low metal gate, which squeaked on dry hinges as he did so, and was, whether by design or not, he thought, a very efficient burglar deterrent. He rapped on the brass knocker, employing the traditional police officer's knock ... tap, tap ... tap. The door was opened rapidly by a slender, healthy looking man who Vicary assessed to be in his late sixties.

'What!' the man demanded, aggressively.

'Police.' Vicary showed the man his ID. 'No trouble, just seeking information.'

'Oh ... I see.' The man instantly relaxed. 'It can get bad round here, kids knocking on doors and then running away. Dare say it could be worse. I moved the old knocker higher up the door but they can still reach it.' The man spoke with a warm London accent. 'And if it's not kids, it's folk trying to sell me double glazing.'

'Well, I'm not either one,' Vicary replied softly. Behind the man he saw a neat, well-ordered hallway with everything just so, and the smell of furniture polish from within the house reached him. He stood on the threshold, but still out of doors. 'Can I ask, are you Mr Halkier?'

'Yes, that I am. Joseph Halkier. Why?'

'Did you report your daughter as a missing person some ten years ago?'

'Yes...' The man's voice seemed to rise in its pitch. 'Yes, our Rosemary. Why?'

'I'm afraid I may have some bad news for you.'

Joseph Halkier stiffened. 'After this length of time, there can be no bad news. If it's about our Rosemary it can only be good news, even if her dear old body has been found that's still good news, because it's better than not knowing.' He stepped aside. 'You'd better come in, sir.'

Vicary stepped over the threshold and wiped his shoes on the 'welcome' mat just inside the doorway. Joseph Halkier, dressed in a blue sweater, jeans and sports shoes – which made him appear younger than his likely years – shut the door behind Vicary with a gentle click and asked him to go into the first room on his right, which transpired to be the living room of the home. It was furnished with a 1950s vintage three-piece suite, heavy 1930s vintage wooden furniture and a dark-brown carpet. The room had a surprisingly musty smell, and that, and the absence of any form of heating, suggested to Vicary that the room was designated to be the 'best' room of the house, used only on special occasions or to entertain official callers. The day-to-day living in the house –

including the television, radio and music player and the heating – was likely to be confined to the rear of the house. Joseph Halkier followed Vicary into the room and indicated the armchairs and the settee, and said, in a sombre, resigned tone, 'Please do take a seat, sir.'

Vicary sat in the armchair which stood furthest from the door so that he had his back to the window as dusk enveloped the street. Halkier sat opposite him in a matching armchair. He remained silent but stared intently at Vicary.

'No easy way of telling you, Mr Halkier, but a body has been found. It is a body which matches the description of Rosemary but ... but I have to say that the identity has to be confirmed.'

Joseph Halkier's head sagged forward. He held it like that for a few moments before recovering. 'I'm glad she isn't here...'

'Sorry?' The reaction astounded Vicary.

'Oh ... no ... sorry...' Halkier stammered, 'don't get me wrong. I mean my wife, Mrs Halkier.'

'I see.'

'She died a year ago without knowing what had happened to Rosemary, but she always lived in hope. Even just before she died she would say things like, "She'll be in a hospital somewhere, not knowing who she is ... lost all her memory, that's why she hasn't contacted us. She'll phone soon, you'll see, just you wait and see ... it happens all the time." I never said anything but ... after a week I knew we'd never see her alive again. It was so not like her to not let us know where she was. But the identification will be positive. Where was she...' Halkier paused, 'where was her body found?'

'Her body – if it is hers – was found on Hampstead Heath.'

'The Heath.' Halkier sighed. 'All these years and she was so close ... as the crow flies ... ten miles, perhaps a little more. That is close considering where she could be, like the north of Scotland, but at least my wife died before she was found. She never gave up hope.' He drew a deep breath. 'So, whereabouts on the Heath?'

'Close to the Spaniards Road entrance.'

'Spaniards Road?'

'Yes. If you go to that entrance you might probably see the remains of blue-and-white tape strung about the bushes. There will be a hollow just inside the shrubs, hidden from view.'

'A hollow ... a shallow grave?'

'Yes,' Vicary replied solemnly, 'it was a shallow grave for someone, a female, possibly mid-thirties, just five feet tall.'

'That's Rosemary.'

'And who has given birth.'

'Again ... that's Rosemary.'

'We still need something to make a positive identification.'

'Such as?'

'A full-face photograph, the name and address of her dentist ... something with her DNA on it ... a sample of your DNA, a sample of her children's DNA.'

'You can have all of them from me, but her ex-husband has custody of the children.'

'Alright, that is not a problem. I will arrange for someone to call tomorrow to collect a sample of your DNA.'

'Very well, I'll also try and find something with her DNA on it.'

'Thank you.'

'I'll wait in ... then I'll go up to the Heath – Spaniards Road entrance?'

'Yes.'

'I'll buy some flowers, then go up there.'

'Yes,' Vicary replied softly for want of something to say. 'Yes, I can understand you wanting to do that.'

'Dare say I'll be going up quite often from now on. What father has two graves to visit for one daughter? I'll visit the one she was in and the one she's going in.'

Vicary remained silent for a moment and then asked, 'Can you tell me anything about her disappearance?'

'Went out ... leaving the children here, and she didn't return. That's it.'

'She was living here at the time – not with her husband?'

'No. She was divorced. We were pleased about that, her husband was no good, a real waster ... he probably still is, and I fear for my grandchildren with him for a father. They live with him in Clacton ... Clacton.' Halkier shook his head slowly. 'He does summer work in the amusement arcades and on the dodgem cars. He lives for the summer, all those bright lights and machines making noises, and in the winter he just mopes about. In his head he's about six years old. Eventually Rose left him and brought the children back here, and she and my wife looked after them. They settled into the school and after a bit of a slow start their school work improved no end. Rose got interim custody of the children, pending the final divorce settlement, and got a job, a telephonist in a call centre; modern day sweatshop she always used to call it but at least it was a wage coming in.'

'Was she seeing anyone at the time she disappeared?'

'I think she was but we never met him. I didn't like the sound of him.'

'Oh?'

'Lived well south of London, large house, but was very cagey about what he did for a living ... always a bad sign.'

'Indeed.'

'But that was our Rosemary, lovely looking girl, just five feet nothing but ... oh so beautiful ... and such a personality, men really went for her. She could have had her pick but would she pick a good man? Just a halfwit who likes amusement arcades and a dodgy sounding character who lives in a huge house in Surrey, and won't tell her how he makes his bundle – total, total, total shtum about that bit. Dodgy.'

'Sounds it.'

'But it was more than casual; she would go to live with him for a week at a time, longer sometimes. Then she took a bag of clothes and just didn't come back. She said she went to work each day from his house.'

'I was going to ask...'

'Yes, well, once her husband found out she had been reported missing, he came up from Clacton on the first old train he could get and took his children back with him. I do fear for them with him as a father.'

'You can't do anything, sir.'

'I know. Just exchange cards at Christmas now; send the children birthday cards as well, and things like book tokens instead of cash, but that's all I can do. I'll go for a pint tonight – that's what I do when I have things to think about, walk to the boozer, then walk the streets.'

'Don't like it.' The man screwed the cigar stub into the large ashtray. 'The Old Bill have found her, that's what they called to tell me. They weren't interested in Irish Mickey Dalkeith, the little toerag; it was that old brass they found under his body. I know it was a bad call telling him to get rid of her body; I should have had more loaf. The Bill just called to tell me they are going to pull me for it.'

'You don't know that.' The woman sat on the settee with her legs folded up beneath her and pulled on a cigarette held in a long, ivory holder. 'You weren't even there, was you?'

'I didn't need to be ... do me a favour ... I didn't need to be. I gave the nod didn't I?'

'Have it your own way, but I reckon you're panicking for nothing.'

'Yeah ... well it ain't your bonce on the old block is it?'

The woman, sensing she was caged with

an angry tiger, picked up a copy of *Cosmopolitan* and hid behind it.

Harry Vicary walked from the Halkier house to Leyton High Road and crossed it at a pelican crossing, and continued down winding Longthorne Road, past the hospital and turned left into Leytonstone High Road. He crossed the high road, also at a pelican crossing. The traffic being heavy by then, and in his opinion the crossings were the only safe way to cross the road after dusk had turned to night; like most police officers who had attended numerous road accidents, Vicary had developed a strong sense of caution. He turned off the main road into quieter Lister Road, enjoying the walk and the peace, and the sense of space that it afforded. He chose to follow Bushwood Road, with thickly wooded Wanstead flats to his right. At that moment, the flats looked bleak and sinister, with the tall, leafless trees standing motionless in the dark, while to his left the homely lights burned in the houses. He turned into Hartley Road and walked up to the front door of the house, which was of similar vintage and design to Joseph Halkier's home. He let himself in and was instantly aware of the silence within the house, and he knew

107

something was amiss.

He found his wife in the front room. She was sitting upright on the settee, quite still but not in any form of resting position. Her eyes were wide open yet she seemed to be registering nothing at all. Vicary groaned. She had been doing so well, so very, very well. They both had. The gin bottle lay on the floor at her feet. Empty. He took his wife and gently pulled her off the settee and laid her on the floor in the recovery position, lest she vomit in her condition, or later, when she had fallen asleep. He took off his coat and phoned his wife's place of work, explaining that she had been taken ill and because of this she would not be at work tomorrow, and probably not the day after either. He placed a frozen pizza in the microwave and ate it quietly with a marked lack of enthusiasm. After he had eaten he searched their house. One bottle would mean, two, or three, or four ... and they would be somewhere she had not used before. Room by room, cupboard by cupboard he searched the house and found them: two bottles of Gilbey's, as he had expected, in a place she had not used before. On this occasion he found them under the eaves in the attic conversion. Beneath the table by the wall was a small one-foot-square doorway used to access the wiring of the house. He opened up the door and one of the bottles fell into his hand; the other was to be seen lying on its side. Both were full and unopened. He emptied the contents into the sink.

Then, like Joseph Halkier, he went out to walk the streets, but unlike Joseph Halkier, he could not, would not, dared not, seek comfort and refuge in a pub.

THREE

Josie Pinder blinked and drew on the cigarette. 'Sorry,' she mumbled, pulling the Bakelite ashtray across the yellow Formica surface of the kitchen table. 'This is a bit early for me.' She pulled the towelling robe around her.

'You'll be able to get back to bed in a while.' DC Brunnie spoke softly but firmly. 'Tell us about the girl in Irish Mickey's room, then you can snuggle up to your mate for a bit more sleep.'

'No, not so lucky, sunshine, I've got to go and see the Gestapo this morning.' She glanced at the inexpensive battery operated travel clock which sat on the narrow window sill. 'In fact, it's probably a good thing that you did bang on the door.'

'The Gestapo?'

'The dole office – if I miss an appointment, they stop my benefit. And they enjoy doing it. They're the bottom of the pile, you see, so they need someone beneath them;

110

that's what Sonya says, you see.'

'I see.'

'So they'll want to know what effort I have been making to find a job.'

'Fair enough.'

'Well, find me a job and I'll do it, I say, but since I have never worked at all ... not one single job since I left local authority school with no qualifications ... I am not a good employment prospect.'

'Never?'

'Nope ... not ever.' She drew heavily on the cigarette and exhaled the smoke through her nostrils. She was small, with short yellow hair. Brunnie thought she was barely over five feet tall and her pale complexion spoke of a poor diet. 'Sonya's the same, she's never worked either, but we get by.'

'Like the way Billy Kemp does? Cash in hand job at the Chinese eatery?'

'Yeah ... but not proper work, we're not paying National Insurance stamps and all that malarkey.'

'So tell us about the girl.'

'Not much to tell.'

'Well that's a damn sight more than we know right now. So tell.'

'She moved in a few weeks ago. Irish Mickey brought her home and she lived in his room while he was at home in north

Palmers Green, I think, with his
Then he moved back here and
he room with her. She was Welsh.'
ı,' Brunnie repeated.
'That's a start.' DC Ainsclough scribbled
'Welsh' on his notepad.
'I had a little chat with her once. She was
from the Cardiff area, she said. She had a
Welsh accent. Very musical the old Welsh
accent, and she used Welsh terms like "tidy"
for "nice" or "good". Once Billy came home
and said he'd got extra hours at the Chinese
restaurant and he'd be lifting more money
that week, and she said, "Oh, there's tidy for
you", and she also said "by here" instead of
"just here" or "in there", like "Is this your
food cupboard by here?"'
'OK ... Welsh.'
'She was a runaway.'
'From home?'
'From a children's home. Irish Mickey
found her in King's Cross; she was trying to
sell herself on the street. He recognized
what she was and he wanted to stop her becoming a brass, so he brought her back
here.'
'You mean he rescued her?' Ainsclough
could not help a note of surprise enter his
voice.
'Yeah, reckon you could say that. That was

112

like Irish Mickey, he had a good old heart; not like him to get caught up with Pilcher.'

'Did you see or hear anything the night she was murdered?'

Josie Pinder tapped the side of her nose. 'I don't mind telling you about her but I don't want to end up like her.'

'If you're withholding information...'

'Hey, I'd rather withhold information and live, rather than give information and not live. This isn't much. I am not much, but it's better than being inside a block of concrete.'

'Pilcher puts people inside concrete?'

'So they say, and he was round here yesterday evening after we got back from the police station. We all got well warned not to go talking to the Old Bill or we'd be on the street ... or worse. He had a couple of soldiers with him.'

'Soldiers?'

'Heavies, ex-soldiers, fit and good at taking orders, all part of his firm. I'm listening to him, so's Sonya and Billy Kemp. He's off like a rabbit out of the old trap.'

'Left?' Brunnie reported.

'Gone,' Ainsclough added, 'left his tenancy?'

'Naw ... he left early to avoid talking to the Old Bill in case they came – and look who it ain't. We should have gone with him I

113

reckon, but try getting Sonya out of her pit. Billy will be sitting all day in the public library, just to keep warm … sensible boy.'

'You're frightened of Pilcher?' Brunnie remarked.

'Oh, it shows does it?' She flicked ash into the ashtray. 'You hear things. He's a nasty piece of work and you don't mess with him, even if half of what is said is true. I mean, he owns property, buys up houses and does them up but…' she worked the cigarette butt into the ashtray. 'Well, rumours is rumours, and all that concrete that goes into foundations can hide a chopped-up body easy-peasy, or a whole one. All those professional tenants in those done-up houses with their cellars – there's lumps of concrete you don't want to take an old pneumatic drill to … so they say. I usually deal with J.J.'

'J.J.?'

'J.J. Dunwoodie, he looks after the office round the corner.'

'Ah, yes, I've met J.J.'

'He seems to like working for Pilcher for some reason, but Billy Kemp might know something that I don't. He was frightened this morning, said J.J. had shot his mouth off about something and we'd better not do the same.'

Ainsclough and Brunnie glanced at each

other, and Brunnie asked, 'When did he say that?'

'This morning, dark and early. I needed to get up and he was making himself some tea and was dressed to go out ... it was like he'd seen an old ghost.'

Ainsclough turned to Brunnie and said, 'We'd better take a swift hike round there.'

'Yes. We came to find out about the Welsh girl though.' Brunnie turned to Josie Pinder, who was grappling another cigarette from the packet. 'What was her name?'

'Gaynor.' Josie Pinder lit the cigarette with a blue disposable lighter.

'Second name.'

'Dunno ... just called herself Gaynor.'

'Did she tell you her age?'

'Naw, but she was under sixteen, she wouldn't have been in a care home otherwise, would she? I mean, stands to reason doesn't it?'

'Fair point,' Brunnie growled. 'Did she go out?'

'Hardly ... Irish Mickey sent her money.'

'He did?'

'Brown envelope arrived for her every now and then. I recognized Irish Mickey's handwriting on the front of the envelope.'

'There was no surname on the envelope?'

'No ... just "Gaynor".'

115

'So she did jobs for Pilcher?'

'Don't think so. Never saw her do no work. Pilcher may not have known she was there.'

'What do you do for Pilcher?'

'We keep the squatters out. It wouldn't be difficult for Pilcher to evict squatters but he'd rather not have them in the first place.'

'Anything else you do for him?'

Again, she tapped the side of her nose. 'You'd better go now if you want us to be safe; Pilcher will be watching this place.'

'He will?'

'Or his goons will. He's frightened of the police.'

'That's interesting.' Ainsclough stood.

'Very, very interesting indeed.' Brunnie also stood. 'We'll be back, but in the interests of your safety, we'll go for now.'

Cold caring. That was the expression. Cold caring. He looked at his wife, so attractive when she cared to be, but now lying on the carpet with her hair matted with her own vomit – she was snoring loudly and so was safe. She would wake soon, feeling frail and cold, and would have such a mess to clean, but all the learned advice said that this was the correct approach. She will not fight the drink unless she wakes up lying in the mess

116

she, and she alone, has created. He walked out of the house, locking the door behind him.

Cold caring. Very cold. Very caring.

Ainsclough and Brunnie walked into the offices of WLM Rents on Fernhead Road, Kilburn. The premises were exactly as Brunnie recalled them from the previous day, but the helpful and, in Brunnie's eyes, slightly sycophantic J.J. Dunwoodie was absent. Instead, a hard-faced blonde of about twenty-five summers sat in the chair he had occupied. She was dressed in black, was very slender, and had eyes of such steel-cold blue that Ainsclough felt a chill run down his spine. Brunnie, alarmed and worried, glanced at the top of the filing cabinets and saw a green, not a red, watering can beside the row of potted plants. He experienced a sinking feeling in the pit of his stomach.

'Mr Dunwoodie,' Brunnie asked, 'is he here?'

'Who wants him?' The woman, immaculately dressed, sat back in her chair, filing her brightly varnished fingernails. Her thin fingers were bedecked with rings; her wrists were encircled by expensive looking bracelets which rattled softly as she worked the

117

file over her nails, occasionally stopping to admire her work. A strong cloud of scent rose from her and reached the officers. She didn't look up as she replied to Brunnie's question.

'Police.'

'You have ID?' Again, she didn't take her eyes off her fingernails.

Ainsclough and Brunnie showed their ID cards and, still without looking up, the woman said, 'OK.' Then she added, 'Mr Dunwoodie don't work here no more, do he?'

'We don't know. Doesn't he?' Brunnie snarled.

'No, he don't. Not since last night he don't. I'm in charge here now ... well, until Mr Pilcher can get a new office manager. I just answer the phone and take messages and if someone comes in looking for a place to rent. I take their name and contact details, and tell them someone will be in touch, but that's only if they're kosher, like all respectable and that, 'cos if they're not kosher they don't rent, not from here anyway. It's a very responsible job. We don't rent to no toerags, though.'

'Seems so,' Ainsclough replied drily. 'So who are you?'

'Felicity Skidmore.'

'So why don't you tell us your real name?'

The young woman glanced up and glared at Brunnie, though she said nothing.

'We need to speak to Mr Dunwoodie.'

The woman admired her nails once again. 'Well, I can't help you, because he's not here, is he?'

'Home address?'

'Don't ask me, darling.'

'You might not know it, but it'll be filed away. Every employer has his workers' home addresses on file.'

'Maybe, but I wouldn't know where it is ... have a look.' She inclined her head towards the bank of filing cabinets.

Ainsclough glanced at the cabinets. He knew it would be a waste of time to look through their contents.

Felicity Skidmore, clearly satisfied, placed her nail file in a large black handbag. 'Look, darling, I just got receptionist skills, nothing more. I got no office skills; don't know nothing about filing or word-processing, nothing. I usually work in another office for Mr Pilcher, don't I, and this morning he hands me the keys and tells me to drive over here and open up for him, and tells me what to do ... answer the phone, take details of the kosher ones and turn the toerags away – but diplomatic like, he don't want his windows

119

put through at night. Just say to them there ain't nowhere to rent.'

'A responsible job, as you say.'

Brunnie asked, 'Where do you normally work?'

'What's that got to do with you?' Felicity Skidmore flushed with indignation. 'Bang out of order is that question. Bang out of order.'

Ainsclough smiled to himself. The legendary East End dislike of the police was emerging from Felicity Skidmore. Blagger, he thought. If Felicity Skidmore is not a blagger herself, then she's a blagger's tart or the daughter of a blagger. Definitely on the other side of the fence.

'It's got a lot to do with us,' Brunnie replied. 'It's got so much to do with us that you could be looking at porridge for obstruction. This is a murder investigation.' Brunnie paused. 'And pretty girls like you are very popular in Holloway. You get traded between the butch dykes for an ounce of tobacco, and you don't get any say in the matter.'

'No say at all,' added Ainsclough. 'If we run you in, we'll do an automatic check for any outstanding warrants and take your dabs to see if we know you under another name. We have plenty of room in the cells.

You can even have one to yourself, but you won't get that luxury in Holloway. Mind you, you probably already know that.'

'I've never been inside!'

'Yet,' Brunnie replied calmly, 'but obstruction in a murder investigation will guarantee the clanging of the door behind little you.'

Felicity Skidmore sighed and folded her arms. 'Continental Imports and Exports.'

'Continental Imports and Exports?' Brunnie repeated.

'That's what I said.'

'What does that outfit import and export?'

'Furniture.'

'Furniture?'

'Yeah, like beds and wardrobes, and tables and chairs, and chests of drawers and that ... furniture. What with the European Community, people are buying houses in Frogland and islands in the old Med ... even in Eastern Europe, and they want their furniture with them ... And the foreigners, they buy in the UK, and they bring their old furniture with them. So Mr Pilcher, he provides a removal service.'

Brunnie and Ainsclough glanced at each other and smiled. 'Furniture,' Brunnie said.

'Furniture,'Ainsclough echoed.

'Well, I ain't seen nothing but furniture going in and out. It's not my fault I'm a looker. I just answer the old dog and bone and set the place off right. I do that at Continental and Mr Pilcher sent me here today to do the same thing.'

'And turning the toerags away.'

'Yeah, that too, but nicely with it. I get that responsibility.'

'So where is Continental Imports and Exports based?'

'Down the Mile End Road. Can't miss it. Near the old junction with Cambridge Heath Road. Big sign. Black letters on yellow background.'

'Did you know Mr Dunwoodie?'

'Nope. It's just the name of the geezer who sat here until yesterday; I don't know no more than that, so help me. I don't know nothing about him or why he isn't here today, but I get a change of scenery and that's as good as a rest, so they say.'

'So what's in the back room?'

'Dunno. Wasn't told and I didn't ask. Them that's asks no questions, gets told no lies.' She smiled at Brunnie. 'It's safer that way, me old china, a lot safer. I wasn't given the key anyway. So if you want to know what's in there, and if you want to know where J.J. Dunwoodie is, you'll have to ask Mr Pilcher, won't you? If he phones, I'll tell him the Old Bill was here. He'll want to know.'

'You do that.'

Walking away from the offices of WLM Rents, Ainsclough said, '"Me old china"? Never did work that one out.'

Brunnie fished in his coat pocket for his car keys. 'China plate – mate. Me old china plate – mate.'

Joseph Halkier seemed to Vicary to shrink into his armchair. He nodded slowly and gently, and then said, 'Thank you for calling on me and telling me in person. It's good of you, I appreciate it. I thought you might send a uniformed constable, you see, so thank you. The DNA was a match. I knew it would be.'

'No thanks are necessary, I assure you.'

'But still ... you know, I knew it would be our Rose. I am not really one for all that other-worldly mumbo-jumbo – never have been one for the paranormal – but I went up to the Heath last night ... I followed your directions and was able to make out the police tape in the dark, well the white bits anyway, and when I got to the tape I felt a link, a bond. I don't have the words, but I felt she was there.'

'A connection?' Vicary suggested.

Halkier smiled 'Yes, that's a good way of

123

putting it ... a connection. I felt a strong connection with that location. I felt that I knew it had been our Rosemary who had lain there all those years. I picked up a bit of soil and took it home with me. That might be a bit morbid but I wanted to do it ... Quite near the road for a shallow grave?'

'Yes. It would have been dug at night, in the summer when the soil would not be frozen.'

'Sorry about the soil but Rose had touched it and I wanted some. I hope I wasn't disturbing a crime scene.'

'No, you did no harm and I don't think it was a morbid act.'

'Thank you. I was worried on those two counts.'

The conversation halted as that day's post clattered though Joseph Halkier's letterbox and fell on to the hallway floor. 'Bills and junk mail, it's all I get these days.'

'Early?'

'Yes, we still get our mail early in the morning, well, mid-morning, not like the six a.m. or seven a.m. deliveries as it was in the old days, but still reasonably early. So how can I help you? I'll help in any way I can. She was my only daughter.'

'Thank you.' Vicary inclined his head to one side. 'Well, we really need to know as much about your daughter's private life as we can, as much as you can tell us ... her friends, associates; any light that you can shed on her day-to-day comings and goings. Was she employed?'

'Yes, in a call centre, phoning folk and trying to make them buy things they don't need. She hated it – modern day version of door-to-door salesmen. Phone sales ... it's ... don't know ... get right into people's houses.'

'I feel the same way,' Vicary replied. 'My wife and I have an answering machine; we keep it on all the time, even when we are at home. The telesales people hang up immediately they hear a recorded voice.'

'That's a good idea. You know, I might buy one ... in fact, I think I will. Well, the call centre ... this was ten years ago now.'

'Appreciate that, but it's a start.'

'It was on the edge of the City, by which I mean the Square Mile.'

'Yes. Understood.'

'I still have the details upstairs.' Joseph Halkier stood with what Vicary thought was impressive effortlessness and suppleness for a man of his years and left the room. Vicary heard him scoop up the post from the floor of the hallway and then listened as he skipped up the stairs. He returned a few

125

moments later with one of Rosemary Halkier's pay advices and a child's exercise book, which had a smiley face sticker on the front. He handed both to Vicary.

'The pay advice will give you the details of her last employer. You're welcome to hang on to it.'

'Thank you.'

'The exercise book is her address book ... that stays here.'

'Of course.'

Halkier resumed his seat. 'But you are welcome to copy down the addresses of her friends.'

'Excellent.' Vicary leafed through the book. It had, he thought, few entries.

'You mentioned her male friend, the businessman who lived south of the river? Is he in here?' Vicary leafed through the exercise book.

'No. I looked. It was one of the first things I did when she was missing, but it all seemed to be the folk I knew; people in this area and that waster of a husband of hers, her children's school and other addresses like the doctors and dentist ... one or two people she got pally with when she was in Clacton. But no businessmen, though she'd be well impressed with money.'

'You think so?'

'Yes, she never had none once she left home. She grew up here ... Leyton. It's alright, we had a roof, we had a full larder, but she really scratched pennies in Clacton trying to survive on whatever he brought home in the summer, then making the dole stretch in the winter, and when she came back here ... well, the money in the call centre wasn't great – long hours, low pay. So after ten years of scrimping and saving, yes, a guy with money would have an appeal for her. I can see that.'

'But you have no idea who he was?'

'Or still is ... no ... no idea at all.'

'Did she have a particular friend who she was close to?'

Halkier paused. 'You could try Pauline North.'

'Pauline North?'

'Yes, she'll be in the address book somewhere.'

Ainsclough leafed through the book. 'Nothing under "P" or "N",' he said.

'She probably kept her address in here–' Halkier tapped the side of his head – 'but her mother still lives in the street. Opposite side of the road, very end of the street ... five or six doors from the end of the street that way–' Halkier pointed to his left – 'bright yellow door.'

'Yellow door. Who is Pauline North?'

'School friend. They were pretty well inseparable when they were children, drifted apart a little when they discovered boys, but picked up with each other again when Rosemary returned from Clacton. I reckon she'd be worth calling on. She'd likely tell Pauline things she wouldn't tell her old man, and I didn't pry.'

'I fully understand.' Vicary paused. 'Did she seem worried at about the time she disappeared?'

'Not that I recall.' Halkier pursed his lips. 'No ... I can't say that she seemed worried, and I think I'd have been able to tell if she was. She wasn't a girl to bottle things up ... so I can say she wasn't worried.'

'Alright.' Vicary glanced round the room. It seemed to him to be marginally less tidy than it was when he had first visited Joseph Halkier, as if he was losing interest in his surroundings, which, Vicary conceded, would be fully understandable. 'So, how long was it before you reported Rosemary as a missing person? That is to say, how long after you last saw her?'

'Nearly a week, as I recall.'

'That's quite a long time ... I mean, if she was living with you.'

'It was the Thursday before the Easter

weekend. She left that morning to go to work. I heard her leave, so the last time I actually saw her was the previous evening. She had packed a weekend bag. She was going away with her man that weekend – leaving from work on Thursday to travel to his house, then returning here on the Tuesday after work. We only started to worry when we got a phone call from the call centre on the Tuesday at about midday; they were asking if Rose was coming into work, because she hadn't phoned in saying she was sick.'

'I see.'

'So we waited and then reported her missing that evening.'

'Yes...'

'A police constable visited and took some details.'

'Yes.'

'Then we had no contact from the police from that day until your visit, sir, by which time Mrs Halkier had passed on.'

'A very long time...'

'A very long time. You'll do all you can, sir?'

'All we can. You have my word.'

Tom Ainsclough entered the name 'Felicity Skidmore' into the computer and her approximate age as 'mid-twenties'. There was no trace of her. 'Not known,' he said.

'There's a surprise,' Brunnie replied. 'I bet you it's an alias.' He continued to run his fingertip down the list of J. Dunwoodies in the London telephone directory. 'I never knew there were so many, and for each entry there will be two or three ex-directory J. Dunwoodies. I once talked to a telephone operator and she told me that if all the domestic numbers were listed, the book would be twice the size it already is ... Lot of these are in the prestigious suburbs; a lot are too far to make travelling to work in Kilburn practical ... oh ... wait...'

'A hit?' Ainsclough glanced up from the computer screen.

'Possibly.' Brunnie picked up his phone, pressed nine for an outside line and then dialled a number. The call was quickly answered by a tearful sounding woman with a shaky voice. Brunnie said, 'Hello, madam, sorry to bother you. This is the Metropolitan Police at Scotland Yard; I am trying to trace a Mr J.J. Dunwoodie who is employed at WLM Rents in Kilburn.'

'Oh ... he's in hospital...'

'Hospital!' Brunnie repeated for the benefit of Ainsclough who began to listen, keenly so.

'The Westminster Hospital,' the woman explained. 'He got set on last night, after work ... two thugs and they hurt him bad ... really bad. And you're the police?'

'Yes.'

'Well you should know about it. There's a copper with him in case he wakes up.'

'I am sorry to bother you. I hope all is well. We clearly had a communication breakdown here. Sorry.' Brunnie replaced the phone. 'Westminster Hospital ... got worked over last night.' He sat back in his chair. 'What have I done?'

'What do you mean?'

Brunnie told Ainsclough about the watering can.

'You believed Pilcher's prints would be on it?'

'Yes ... whatever his name is ... his prints would be on the can. I told Dunwoodie to get an identical one from the local shop, but I noticed a green one there this morning, not a red one.'

'That's a bit of an offside thing to do, especially for you.'

'I know, we can't use it to arrest him for anything but at least we'll know who he is.'

'Yes, I know. It's one thing to take fingerprints after a break-in ... even from the staff ... we can tell them it's so they can be elimi-

131

nated, but it gets names and prints on file for future reference. If all the totally innocent citizens whose prints are on file knew about it, there'd be riots in London.'

'I honestly thought he'd be safe. I thought it would be so simple for him to get another red watering can.'

Ainsclough rested his chin in the cup of his left palm, with his elbow resting on the surface of his desk, 'You'd better go straight to Harry Vicary, the moment he gets in.'

'Yes ... that's the best thing to do ... best thing to do rather than let it emerge, but if Dunwoodie registers a complaint, and I wouldn't blame him if he does, I'm up the creek without a paddle. Disciplinary procedures ... the lot. Oh boy, he could even sue the police.'

'But only if he can show the assault was connected to him handing over the watering can. The assault might be unconnected.'

'Good point.' Brunnie smiled at Ainsclough. 'I can live in hope. I think I'd like to get over to Westminster Hospital.'

'Yes. I'll cover for you. Penny Yewdall is in as well, enough plain clothes if anything develops, and we have your mobile phone number. Swannell is still on leave, but it's enough.'

'Yes.' Brunnie stood. 'I'll walk round

there, quicker than taking a car, no place to park anyway. But what have I done?'

Harry Vicary knocked gently on the yellow door of the house at the far end of Albert Road, Leyton, E10. An elderly lady opened the door, silver-haired, floral dress, hands twisted with arthritis. 'Mrs North?' Vicary took off his hat and replaced it again.

'Yes.' Her voice was shaking with apprehension.

'Police.' Vicary smiled. 'Don't be alarmed.'

'Ah.' Mrs North relaxed and smiled.

Vicary produced his identity card. 'I understand you have a daughter, Pauline.'

'I did.'

'Oh ... I am sorry.'

'No, no ... still alive.' Mrs North smiled. 'She's Mrs South now.'

'You're joking,' Vicary grinned.

'I kid you not, young man. The jokes they made at the wedding reception, about compass needles spinning round until North became South ... Go North, young man ... I can't remember them all, but one telegram after the other had some crack in it about points of the compass. The best man was the groom's brother but they managed to find an usher called West and another called Eastman – it became a theme of the wedding.'

'How amusing.'

'Yes. She did well; her husband is a good man and she has two lovely children.'

'I am pleased to hear it. I really would like to speak to her. She has nothing to worry about; I need to pick her brains.'

'She's not in trouble?'

'No. I just need information.'

'Alright ... well if you don't mind, I'll phone her and ask her to contact you.'

'Of course.' Vicary handed her his calling card.

Mrs North read the card. 'Detective Inspector Vicary. That's quite a high rank.'

'Not really. It's quite modest.'

'Can I tell her what it is about?'

'Yes, I don't see why not, it's in connection with Rosemary Halkier.'

'Oh ... Rose ... she disappeared.'

'Yes.'

'Has she been found?'

'Well, let's just say that there has been a significant development. If you could invite your daughter Pauline to phone me at her earliest convenience?'

'I will ... yes, I will. I'll phone her right away; she doesn't work. I mean, she's not employed during the day, she keeps house when she is not needed for supply teaching

134

and that's sufficient work for any woman ... but if she isn't at home now, she'll be out somewhere close by ... at the shops or something.'

'I see.'

'She lives in Mill Hill. Well, I'll phone her. Will you be going direct to Scotland Yard, sir?'

'No ... no ... I have another call to make first.'

Vicary walked home. He was anxious to get there, but he did not want to lessen the impact of the cold caring policy. He reached his house and let himself in. His wife was on her hands and knees cleaning the vomit from the carpet with her head wrapped in a towel. Clearly she had washed herself first. She looked at him and then avoided eye contact. After a period of silence he asked, 'Is there any more? I found the bottles under the eaves. You know we made an agreement. So, is there any more?'

'In the garden.' She spoke with clear difficulty. Even from the distance he stood from her, he could smell her searing breath. 'Behind the shed.'

Vicary walked to the kitchen and out into the back garden. He looked behind the garden shed and found a metal bucket covered with a generous amount of sacking. Neither the bucket, which was shiny and new, nor the sacking, which was old and worn, had he seen before. He took the sacking from the bucket and exposed three more bottles of gin contained within the bucket. He opened each bottle, and holding it away from him and with his head turned from it, lest he got a whiff which he would find difficulty in resisting, he emptied the contents on to the ground. Holding the bottles as far from him as he could, he took them into the kitchen and rinsed each one clear of any trace of alcohol. He then placed them in a plastic bin liner, and went back outside and picked up the screw tops from each bottle, and those too he rinsed and put in the bin liner, which he secured with a firm knot at the top.

He stood silently in the kitchen wondering if he should make his wife a cup of strong black coffee, but he decided against it. He said not a word, and walked out of the house carrying the bin liner with him, which he would place in the first waste bin he came across.

Cold caring.

DC Frank Brunnie walked into the front entrance of the Westminster Hospital and enquired at the reception desk as to the whereabouts of patient J.J. Dunwoodie. Following the directions given, he took the stairs, rather than the ease of the lift, to the given floor, and walked along the corridor, which had a light-fawn coloured floor and cream-painted walls, busy nurses scurrying about and aloof doctors who moved more leisurely, but who were equally serious in their attitude. It had that distinct smell which Brunnie could never analyse. It smelt ... just like a hospital. He saw a police constable sitting on a chair outside a private room. The constable stood defensively as Brunnie approached him. 'Help you, sir?' he asked coldly.

'Alright–' Brunnie showed the constable his ID – 'I'm in the club.'

'Oh ... sorry, sir, didn't recognize you.' He was young, early twenties Brunnie guessed.

'No worries. What happened?'

'Don't know a right lot, sir.' The constable spoke with a distinct Lancashire accent; a young man taking the opportunity through his employment to live in London for a few years, as do many teachers and other public and civil servants, before returning to the provinces and their roots, where housing is affordable. 'I am told not to allow anyone in except hospital staff and the interested officer, sir.'

137

'Who is?'

'DC Meadows, Kilburn nick, sir.'

'I see. DC Meadows...' Brunnie committed the name and workplace to memory, noting that he knew a Meadows once – the name would be easy to remember because of it. 'I'll take a drive over to Kilburn.' He nodded to the door. 'How is he ... the patient?'

'Unconscious, sir, all wired up like I don't know what. I think he was worked over and left for dead, so I heard, but I wasn't told that. I'm just here to make sure no one goes in apart from those what should go in, those what has a right to go in, sir.'

'Someone wanted him dead?'

'Sounds like, sir.'

'He must be in a bad way.'

'Not moving ... and I heard one of the doctors say that it was a miracle he was still alive and that he must have a right strong will to live, but he's a long way to go before he's out of danger.'

'That was said?'

'Yes, sir, the doctor was explaining the situation to the nursing team and I was standing there in the background, like, but I heard him say that. This must be more than a random attack in the street, otherwise I would not be here to protect him, would I?'

'Probably not. DC Meadows of Kilburn nick, you say?'

'Yes, sir.'

Harry Vicary easily found the call centre. It still occupied the same premises as it did when Rosemary Halkier was employed therein, and still had the same business name. He pushed open the glass front door of the building and walked across deep carpeting to the reception desk. The receptionist's smile was broad, with teeth that could sell toothpaste, and, like an air hostess who does not want to be flying again so soon, utterly disingenuous. She wore loud scarlet lipstick and had her blonde hair tied back in a ponytail. 'Can I help you, sir?'

'Police.' Vicary showed the young woman his ID. The reception area smelled powerfully of air freshener and polish, so much so that Vicary felt overwhelmed. The absence of even a plant in a pot did not surprise him.

'Oh...'

'I would like to talk to a senior person ... the manager ... the personnel officer, someone who can tell me about staff here, longserving staff.'

'Yes, sir, please take a seat.' The woman picked up a brown-coloured phone off her desk, pressed four numbers and relayed

Vicary's request, and then said, 'Yes, alright. I will.' She smiled another broad 'I'm only doing this job for the money' smile at Vicary and said, 'Mr Perkins will see you directly, sir.'

Vicary, his hat resting upon his crossed knees, inclined his head in thanks. He and the woman then proceeded to sit in an awkward silence, and Vicary sensed from the young woman's embarrassment that it was clear she had nothing to do all day but receive visitors and answer the telephone, with not even a colleague or two to talk with. Being photogenically attractive clearly had its downside. Moments of awkward silence elapsed and then the door at the side of the reception area was opened, and a short man in a sports jacket and cavalry twill trousers stood in the doorway. Vicary thought him to be mid-thirties. He had a businesslike manner about him, and upon his entrance the receptionist lowered her head slightly as if making a careful study of her desktop. She was evidently intimidated by him and perhaps, Vicary pondered, the reception area, being out of the way, was the safest place for her.

'Police?' The man was clean-shaven with piercing eyes.

Vicary stood, 'Yes, Detective Inspector

Vicary, New Scotland Yard.'

'Scotland Yard? Must be serious.'

'Murder and Serious Crime Squad.' Vicary showed Perkins his ID. 'Doesn't get more serious.'

'How can we help you, sir?'

'I need information about your staff.'

'Anyone in particular?'

'Rosemary Halkier.'

'Halkier ... Halkier ... I confess that name doesn't ring any bells but I have only been here for six weeks; I was headhunted from Thames Bridges.'

'Thames Bridges?'

'Oh ... a rival company.'

'I see, well you won't know her, she used to work here but that was about ten years ago.'

'Ten years!' Perkins gasped. 'We might have some documentation. We have a few long-staying staff but most go after a few months. The only person who is likely to be able to help you is Mrs Maas, she deals with our personnel, and she's been here for a long time.'

'She sounds ideal. Mrs Mars, like the planet?'

'Pronounced the same but not spelled the same.' Perkins corrected Vicary on the spelling of the lady's name. 'I'll take you to her.'

Perkins led Vicary up a narrow stairway of unsurfaced breeze-block walls. On the first floor the workers sat in small cubicles, each isolated from the other, each with a headset rather than a hand-held phone, each in front of a computer screen and keyboard. Perkins walked quietly by. With working conditions like this, Vicary thought, the call centre could aptly be described as a modern day sweatshop. Perkins led Vicary across the open-plan area of the call centre operations room, humming with voices, and opened a door at the far end, which led on to an area of individual offices. He walked to an office on the left-hand side, tapped once on the door and opened it. 'Mrs Maas, this is a Mr Vicary...'

'Pleased to meet you.' Mrs Maas was middle-aged, portly and with a ready smile, which, unlike the isolated receptionist's, Vicary thought, was a genuine smile.

'Mr Vicary is with the police.'

'Oh...' Mrs Maas looked worried.

'I will leave you,' Perkins said to Vicary, 'I have work to address. If anyone can help you, it's Mrs Maas.' And with that, in a brisk about-turn, he left the office, pulling the door shut behind him.

Mrs Maas indicated a vacant seat in her office. 'He's new,' she explained. 'He's very efficient. He was headhunted and is anxious to prove the great and good made the right choice, bless him.'

'So he told me.'

'So ... police?'

'Yes, Scotland Yard, Murder and Serious Crime Squad.' Vicary read the room – neat, efficient, no natural light, very sweatshop-like.

'Murder!'

'Well, yes ... but as I said to Mr Perkins, ten years on, and so this is a bit of a long shot, in fact it's one hell of a long shot, but they've paid off before. We are interested in finding out as much as we can about a lady who used to work here, a lady employee by the name of Halkier, Rosemary Halkier ... home address in Palmers Green.'

'Ten years...' Mrs Maas relaxed. 'You know there might be one or two still here who were here ten years ago; seems that you move on quickly or you work your way into the bricks.' She swivelled on her chair and slowly tapped at her computer keyboard. 'If we search for all current employees with more than ten years' service, and there won't be many ... and the not many is ... five. I count five names, all women, who do tend to stay longer than men.'

'Oh?'

'Flexible hours – they can work round school commitments and work on weekends, leaving hubby to watch the baby. Not a few say that working here keeps them sane, gives them the break they need from demanding children and demanding spouses, and we pay quite well for a call centre. The work is tedious but not demanding. Mr Perkins is keeping them well at it but it's still easier than unskilled work, and it's better than the dole. We pay basic plus commission. The harder you work, the more you earn, and we tell them, you don't just work for yourself or your family, you work for the person next to you; if this company sinks the work could be relocated overseas.'

'I know what you mean,' Vicary replied drily. 'Telephone directory enquiries is now located in the Philippines.'

'Exactly.' Mrs Maas raised her eyebrows. 'And national rail enquiries are in India. So if the crew want to keep the jobs in the UK, they work for each other.' She stood. 'I'll go and chat to the five names, see if any remember. Sorry, who are you enquiring about? My memory...'

'Oh, yes, Rosemary Halkier, lived with her parents in Palmers Green, had two children, short girl, just five foot tall with dark hair.'

'Rosemary Halkier ... Rosemary Halkier.'

Mrs Maas left the office repeating the name to herself, trailing a heavy cloud of perfume behind her. She turned and pointed to a white coffee machine which stood on a table in the corner of her room. 'Do help yourself to coffee.' She smiled. 'It doesn't taste anything like coffee but it's hot and fluid.' She turned again and was gone.

'No thanks,' Vicary replied to an empty room.

Mrs Maas returned some five minutes later in the company of a woman in her forties, who seemed curious and also pleased for the break in her day that Vicary's visit had caused. 'This is Sandra Winthrop. Do take a seat, Sandra.' Mrs Maas sat behind her desk, as Sandra Winthrop sat in a chair adjacent to Vicary. They smiled and nodded at each other.

Mrs Maas opened the discussion. 'Well, it seems you have good fortune and also bad fortune, Mr Vicary. Mrs Winthrop here tells me that while she remembers Rosemary Halkier, perhaps the person you really need to talk to is on sick leave, so she is accessible but not at this location. I took the liberty of phoning her and she says she would be pleased to receive you, but you will have to visit her.'

'Not a problem,' Vicary replied, 'but if she

145

is unwell…'

Mrs Mass smiled 'Broken arm, so not unwell as such.'

'Ah … I see.' Vicary turned to Mrs Winthrop. 'You knew Rosemary Halkier?'

'Yes.' Sandra Winthrop was a warm-faced woman with short black hair. She wore a blue blouse and a long blue skirt.

'Well?'

'No, sir, not very well at all. The person whom you need to talk to more than I is Rachel Pontefract, as Mrs Maas has just indicated.'

'The lady with the broken arm?'

'Yes, she was Rachel Graff in those days but she knew Rosemary very well. They were very good friends. They were known as the "Rolls-Royce Crew", double "R", you see … Rachel and Rosemary.'

'Got you.'

'I was a sort of hanger-on. The three of us went for a drink after work each Friday. We called it the "Friday Club".'

'Alright, I am particularly interested in her life outside her employment. Any male friend you know of?'

'She was separated.'

'Yes, I know that, but we believe she had a male friend.'

'She did have a significant other, yes. He

lived in the south.'

'The south?'

'South of the river. He wasn't married and that attracted Rosemary because her husband wasn't much of a provider ... but her enthusiasm seemed to wane.'

'Really...? That is interesting.'

'So it appeared. Initially, she was very enthusiastic about this fella, but then she seemed preoccupied, as if good living came at an unexpected price, as if she was worried about what she had got herself into.'

'Did she elaborate?'

'Not to me, but she might have taken Rachel Pontefract into her confidence.'

'We'll find out, I dare say. Did she mention a name?'

'Again, not to me, but her worry ... and it might have been fear she was experiencing ... it seemed genuine. It was about that time that she disappeared.'

'Did you tell the police that?'

'No.'

'No?'

'No. I was never asked, none of us were, she was a missing person, so there was no investigation.'

'Of course, we would only investigate missing children.'

'Why the interest now, may we know?'

147

Mrs Maas glanced at Sandra Winthrop and then at Vicary.

'Yes ... her body has been found. There has been a partial press release about a body found on Hampstead Heath.'

'Oh ... I saw that.'

'All London did.' Mrs Maas sighed. 'But she was unidentified.'

'She has now been identified. Her next of kin have been informed and we will be making another press release in which we will name her and ask for information. If you could let me have Mrs Pontefract's contact details?'

'Of course,' Mrs Maas replied with a shaking voice.

Frank Brunnie travelled to Kilburn police station. He entered by the main public entrance and went to the enquiry desk, where he showed his ID to the duty constable and asked for DC Meadows. Two minutes later he and Meadows were walking down the CID corridor towards the detective constable's room. Upon entering the rectangular room, Brunnie noticed that it was crowded with desks, some occupied, others vacant, but all appeared to be in use. Meadows led Brunnie down to the far corner of the room and sat at a desk, and then pointed to the opposite desk. 'Take that seat, please, that guy's in Tenerife right now.'

'That's a coincidence.'

'Oh?'

'Yes, my detective sergeant is due back from there soon – tomorrow, possibly.' Brunnie sank into the chair. 'He says it makes sense to go to Tenerife at this time of the year.'

'That I can readily go along with, Tenerife and the Med are too damned hot in the summer, but January and February, well, they're pleasant months to go south of the fiftieth parallel. I learned the hard way – went to Crete in June once a few years ago, spent the days aching for the night to come, then you only had mosquitoes to deal with ... but the temperature became bearable. So, what brings New Scotland Yard to our little hole?'

'J.J. Dunwoodie.'

'Oh, you have an interest?'

'Well...' Brunnie glanced round the office. Neat and functional, he thought. 'Well, yes and no. What I mean by that is that we have little or no interest in him, but more with his employer.'

'WLM Rents?'

'Yes.' Brunnie paused. 'And I fear I may be responsible for the attack on him.'

'Oh?'

'Yes. If you tell me what happened, I'll tell you why I may be responsible.'

'Simply, the poor lad got duffed up. I mean, well duffed up ... well and truly rolled.'

'Yes, I visited the hospital. You have him under police protection.'

'Yes.' Meadows opened a case file. 'We have a witness to the incident. Too frightened to talk, certainly too frightened to give a statement or go into the witness box, and she also seemed to have something to hide. I mean, this is Kilburn, if it breathes it's probably known to the police.'

'Oh, I thought it was getting gentrified, that's what WLM Rents are pursuing – extending the concept of Maida Vale and Hampstead to include Kilburn.'

'If that's the case, then take it from me, they still have a long way to go. In the evenings the streets round here are still full of urinating Irish women or brawling Irish men.'

'I'll take your word for it.'

'Anyway, the witness, a young black female, saw Dunwoodie being bundled into an alley at the end of his working day yesterday. It was dark by then, and two huge geezers set on little J.J. Dunwoodie.'

150

'I see.'

'They proceeded to give him a right hiding and this wench, the witness, was watching as the turn went down. She was a few feet away, hiding behind a wheelie bin. She was skip-dipping, looking for food. The supermarket dumps all its goods that are past the sell-by date into the wheelie bins in that alley.'

'Yes...'

'If they can, they give it to hostels and the Salvation Army and such like, but they have to do that before midnight of the sell-by date – just one day beyond the sell-by date and it goes into the skip. It's still perfectly edible, but in these claim-culture days no chances are taken. Such a waste, it annoys me.'

'Yes,' Brunnie said again. 'Just twelve hours flying time to Ethiopia, where folk are starving, and we chuck food out, and do so in massive quantities. Madness.'

'So that's what our witness was doing – living a feral existence, tearing into packets of teacakes she had found in the skip, when she saw Dunwoodie getting kicked. In the gloom she was well camouflaged – she is black, like I said, Afro Caribbean – and had on dark clothing: shoes, trousers, jacket, hat ... all dark. She shrank into the shadows and waited till they had finished, and then she phoned us.'

Brunnie smiled. He enjoyed Meadows' dry sense of humour.

'Anyway, she is crouching there frozen with fear, and when it seems safe, she phones us. Good lass ... good for her ... anyone else would have scarpered, just melted into the night and left him to die, or left him for someone else to find, whichever happened sooner. We got there with the paramedics and they put him straight into the ambulance and took him to the Westminster Hospital. We spoke to the witness and she said she heard one of the attackers say, "That's it. He's dead".' Meadows consulted the case file. 'And the second attacker she heard say, "We'd better make sure", to which the first attacker said, "He's dead I tell you, no one could survive that. I've done this before, Rusher, so have you", to which the first attacker, one "Rusher", said, "The boss was clear, he wants him chilled", to which the second attacker apparently said, "He's chilled, let's get off the pitch. We have to get well clear."'

'Hence the protection?'

Meadows nodded. 'Hence the protection. This was no random attack. We'll wait until he wakes up and then see what he can tell us. So where does New Scotland Yard fit in?'

'In respect of his boss, who gives his name as William Pilcher. We have good reason to believe William Pilcher is involved with the murder of the woman whose body was found in a shallow grave on Hampstead Heath.'

'Interesting ... I read the report in the *Evening Standard*; heard about it on Radio London as well.'

'So we want to talk to him a bit more. He lives in a pile in Virginia Water ... some pile ... I mean, a serious pile.'

'Virginia Water? It would be very handsome; only big money camps in Virginia Water.'

'We visited, and believe me, one copper to another, he had "nasty" written all over him.'

'I know what you mean, squire, I well know what you mean.'

'He hummed of suspicion ... reeked like you wouldn't believe ... or maybe you would believe. Ran a trace but we have no record of him, not by the handle he gave.'

'I see.'

'So...' Brunnie shuffled in his chair, leaning forward with hunched shoulders, 'this is where it gets uncomfortable...'

'Go on, you're among friends.'

'I ... well ... a colleague and I visited yesterday, looking for something he had touched ... Pilcher had touched during one of his visits to WLM Rents.'

'To get his prints?'

'Yes.'

'Unorthodox but it happens all the time.'

'Yes ... I know ... I know ... but not with these consequences. You can't use the prints obtained in that way to prosecute but you can identify the person concerned – let's us know who we are dealing with. Anyway, it turns out that Pilcher is a bit of a green-fingered sort of geezer – a lot of nasties have a soft side ... dogs, cats, pigeons. It seems that in Pilcher's case, he likes plants, and he waters the potted plants in the offices of WLM Rents with a little red watering can...' Brunnie took a deep breath. 'So I bullied J.J. Dunwoodie into letting me take the watering can away and told him to get another one, an identical one; told him his boss would be no wiser. He said he couldn't do it, and I said he could and took the can. Called this morning to find that he had been replaced by a hard-nosed looker who works in another of Pilcher's little enterprises – an import/export outfit down the East End. She was there filing her claws 'cos Dunwoodie had "gone sick", she said. Then

154

I saw a green watering can.'

'Oh...' Meadows caught his breath. 'I see your problem.'

'Yes, so at some point Pilcher visited, probably noticed the red can had been replaced by a green one and asked questions, and Dunwoodie told him. Dunwoodie seemed to worship Pilcher for some reason. He might even have told him about the watering can before Pilcher noticed it had been replaced.'

'Not good.'

'Not good at all; not good for Dunwoodie's health, not good for my promotion prospects and very not good for my conscience. I have made a few mistakes I have to live with and I am trying not to accumulate any more.'

'Reckon we are all in the same boat on that score.'

'So if Pilcher is a nasty, and I believe he is, he'll want a victim ... and I—'

The phone on Meadows' desk warbled. He let it ring twice, and then picked it up, identified himself and listened attentively, a worried look appearing on his face as he did so. Eventually he said, 'Thank you, you'd better get back here.' He replaced the handset gently. 'Well, Pilcher got his victim alright.'

'He's dead!'

'Yes, they called it about ten minutes ago – massive heart attack brought on by the assault.'

'So it's murder?'

'Yes.' Meadows sat back in his chair. 'We'll be passing the file to your boys now.'

'Yes, but I'd better come clean with my boss.'

'There's things we have to do yet, so you'll have time ... wrap up the paperwork, get a copy of the death certificate, notify his widow.'

'Yes, that will give me time.'

'I'll have to record your visit. I'll say you were enquiring about his employer, but anything about the watering can and removal of same—'

'Don't compromise yourself, so record what it was I told you ... everything.'

'If you're sure?'

'Yes, I am sure. I'll get to my governor first; make sure he has the full S.P. before the file arrives.'

'But he gave you the can ... Dunwoodie I mean ... he gave you the watering can.'

'Yes, though it was more in the manner of me bullying him into letting me take it.'

'But he did not prevent you from taking it, or say you could not remove it from the

156

premises.'

'No ... no he didn't.'

'Reckon you're covered. If he was stupid enough to tell his governor what had gone down, then it's his lookout.'

Brunnie stood. 'Even so, even so. I'd better go back to the Yard and talk to my governor.'

Tom Ainsclough glanced at the computer screen and smiled, 'Well, well, well, that's a turn up for the books and no mistake.'

'What is?' Penny Yewdall turned away from the window, where she had been pondering the dull, overcast weather which had settled, stubbornly it seemed to her, over London town, and smiled at Ainsclough. 'What's a turn up?'

'Pilcher. Frankie Brunnie's guess was correct, he is a felon.'

'The prints from the watering can?'

'The prints from the watering can ... and I mean, is he known or is he known?'

Yewdall walked from the window and sat in her chair opposite Ainsclough's desk. 'Tell me,' she said.

'Yates ... he is yclept Curtis Yates.'

'That name rings bells.'

'So it should. He's done time ... murder reduced to manslaughter ... he got out after doing five of a ten stretch; that's what you

157

get for volunteering to clean the toilets and joining the Christian Union.'

'Cynic.' Yewdall smiled. 'Probably quite true but you're a cynic just the same.'

'He was part of a team who robbed a security van taking a payroll to a large company – killed a security guard. Poor guy had only been in the job for a few weeks. That was fifteen years ago. He's been off the radar since then but he's flagged up as being of "great interest" – believed to be behind a lot of high-profile jobs in the Greater London area.'

'Mr Big?'

'Seems to be.' Ainsclough continued to read the computer screen. 'His wife disappeared shortly after he was released from Wandsworth ten years ago.'

'That's also about the time Rosemary Halkier disappeared.' Penny Yewdall sat back in her chair and absent-mindedly straightened out a paper clip.

'So it is, both women went missing at the same time. He has a neat way of getting rid of unwanted partners. Oh, my ... one Charlotte Varney ... she was reported missing before he went to prison, but she is cross-referenced to him because she was his partner at the time.'

'Three women!'

'One of whom is known to have been murdered. There's a long list of criminal associates, one of which is none other than Slick Eddie "The Dog" Vasto and another is "Fulham Fred" Morrissey.'

'Eddie "The Dog" Vasto – he was believed to be responsible for the building society job down in Kent a few years ago, I'm sure it was him.'

'It was. Twenty million smackers and it's still missing – won't turn up now it's been well laundered – and if I am right, "Fulham Fred" Morrissey was thought to be the brains behind the bullion robbery at Stansted Airport. If he's moving in circles like that, explains why he doesn't like coppers.'

'What explains who doesn't like coppers?' Frank Brunnie entered the room, peeling off his raincoat as he did so.

'This does.' Ainsclough jabbed a finger in the air towards the monitor screen. 'Your guess was right ... well done.'

Brunnie stood beside Ainsclough, bent forward and read the screen. 'I see ... I see...' he murmured, 'a breakthrough, but I have little to smile about.'

'Why? You got a result.'

'Possibly, but it was at the cost of an innocent seeming office manager being battered to death.' He sank into his chair.

'Who?' Yewdall gasped.

Brunnie told Yewdall and Ainsclough about J.J. Dunwoodie, and a silence fell on the room. Eventually Yewdall said, 'But he let you take it. I said in the car that I wasn't happy with what you did, but he didn't protest or put up any objection. I witnessed that. Alright, you pressured him, but he still allowed you to remove the watering can from the office.'

'That's true, but I am still pushing the envelope of reasonable conduct ... fair play. I am going to have to tell Harry Vicary. Is he in?'

'No.'

'When is he due to return?'

'Not known. May not be until tomorrow now, he's making enquiries in respect of Rosemary Halkier.'

'Alone?'

'Just background information – not interviewing anyone as such.'

'Ah ... I need a drink ... how I need a drink.'

'We got a second result while you were out.' Yewdall patted her notepad.

'Oh?'

'South Wales Police contacted us. They suggested the ID of the murdered girl in Michael Dalkeith's room in the house in

Claremont Road, Kilburn.'

'Oh?' Brunnie repeated.

'A fifteen-year-old runaway from a children's home in Pontypool; they're sending her prints to us.'

'Prints?'

'Yes, she has priors for shoplifting. She is confirmed as being one Gaynor Davies; couldn't get more Welsh than that. Older than John Shaftoe thought. She must have been a waif of a lassie. So where does she fit into the mix, I wonder?'

'If she does fit in anywhere, or at all; her murder might be incidental.'

'Or fitting Dalkeith up?' Yewdall added.

'Who knows?' Brunnie stood. 'But since Harry's not here, I'm going for that beer. I need it.'

Tom Ainsclough alighted from the train at Clapham and walked across Clapham Road, using the pelican crossing, and into Landar Road. Walking on the right-hand pavement, he passed the newly rebuilt Lambeth Hospital and turned right into Hargwyne Street, which he found, as always, to be a pleasingly homely road of nineteenth-century terraced housing, though many, like his, had been converted into two, or sometimes three, separate flats. He stepped up to

161

the front door, opened it with his key and entered the communal hall. He checked the tabletop for mail, and walked to the right-hand door of two internal doors, both of which were secured by mortise locks. He unlocked the door, which opened on to a narrow staircase that led to the upper two storeys of the house; the other, left-hand, door opened on to the ground floor and the cellar, which had been turned into a comfortable bedroom area of three separate rooms. Tom Ainsclough considered himself lucky to have the downstairs neighbour he had. The Watsons both worked in the health-care field – he was a pharmacist at the hospital and she a nurse at the clinic attached to the hospital. Ainsclough lived upstairs with his wife, Sara, a nurse, although she was a staff nurse at the hospital itself. Each family entertained the other for drinks at Christmas time, but otherwise kept themselves to themselves, and made certain to keep any noise they might generate to a minimum. When they met in the communal hall or passed in the street, the greetings were warm and convivial. Tom Ainsclough often envied the Watsons' short walk to the hospital, and his wife's also. But he had more of a sense of being 'at home', because, unlike them, he did not have to look at his place of work each time he glanced out of the rear window of his flat. He entered the kitchen, and he and his wife greeted each other with a brief hug. Ainsclough changed out of his suit and into jeans and a rugby shirt, and relaxed in front of the television, sipping a chilled lager which had been pressed into his hand by a smiling Sara Ainsclough. Later they shared a meal in relaxed silence, punctuated by an occasional comment or two. At nine p.m., Sara excused herself and changed into her nurse's uniform, and after kissing her husband goodbye, she left the house to walk to the hospital in good time to start the night shift at ten p.m. Ainsclough glanced at the framed photograph of himself and Sara taken for them by a stranger whilst on their honeymoon in Crete. The photograph had become a favourite, capturing, he thought, the bliss of those two weeks, and Ainsclough often wondered whether it was the nature of their marriage – the passing each other at the door, and spending the night together only when their shifts allowed them to do so – that was the reason why they remained so content.

Penny Yewdall left the train at Maze Hill Station and turned right into Maze Hill, over the railway bridge, and walked slowly down towards Trafalgar Road, which, at that time of the evening, was log jammed with traffic. She walked down Woodland Crescent and into Tusker Road. She let herself into a small terraced house, just one room downstairs, which served as a sitting room and dining area, with a guest bed under the stairs, and a small yard enclosed by a high fence to the rear of the house. She went upstairs and undressed, and soaked in a bath, as was her wont – unless she felt dangerously sleepy – so as to wash the day off her. She dined at mid-evening and later went for a stroll along the side of Greenwich Park. That she was a policewoman and trained in self-defence made her feel more unafraid than most women would be in such circumstances, but Greenwich being Greenwich, she never had to put her training to use. She returned to her modest house, made a cup of cocoa and had an early night. Her house was small, but it was hers. She liked it like that, and she liked it like that in Greenwich. She felt that no other part of London would work for her the way Greenwich worked for her.

The man and the woman held hands and stood up in the hushed room. The man spoke. He said, 'Hello, we are Harry and Kathleen and we are alcoholics.'

The people in the room answered, 'Hello Harry and Kathleen.'

FOUR

DS Victor Swannell eased his bulk gently into Harry Vicary's office and sat with controlled ease in the vacant chair between Ainsclough and Yewdall, and, looking to his left and right, said, 'Hello, nice to be back.'

Vicary smiled. 'Nice to have you back, and how you are needed. Things have been developing whilst you've been away.'

'I'm all ears, sir.' Swannell sipped his tea.

Vicary briefed him on the case so far and then moved on to more recent developments.

'Now, Frank came to see me this morning and there is an issue which may come to something: we have ascertained Pilcher is aka Curtis Yates.'

Vicary held eye contact with Swannell.

'Not *the* Curtis Yates,' Swannell gasped.

'Yes, the very same.'

'The Metropolitan Police have been after him for years ... murder ... money laundering ... drug smuggling. He's been quiet for a long time. Didn't he go down? He collected a ten stretch for manslaughter.'

'Yes.' Vicary raised his mug of tea to his lips. 'Came out in five and seemed to have dropped off the radar.'

'Well, if I know Curtis Yates, that just means he has been getting someone else to do his dirty for him. He has his enforcers.'

'Seems so, because the employee of WLM Rents who permitted an item to be removed from the premises of the offices of WLM Rents was rolled the other night ... fatally so. Not just a random attack, because we apparently have a witness who claims she heard one of the attackers address the other as "Rusher", and who also heard Rusher say "the boss wants him dead".'

'Rusher,' Swannell repeated the name, 'that handle rings bells.'

'You know Curtis Yates?'

'Yes, I investigated the death of a woman called Charlotte Varney ... I was on that team, anyway.'

'You did?'

'Yes, murdered ... some connection with Yates. We came up against a wall of silence and the case went cold. I would like to think it is going to be warmed up again. We'll have to dig the file out, but if Yates is involved, he'll be getting his crew to do his dirty, like

167

I said, and they'll all be too frightened to grass him up.'

'Always the same,' Ainsclough groaned. 'The big fish make themselves untouchable unless they slip in some way.'

'Yes...' Vicary took up his ballpoint pen and held it poised over his notebook. 'We have three murders now, possibly a fourth if we include Charlotte Varney. We have the murder of Rosemary Halkier, Gaynor Davies, J.J. Dunwoodie ... and Charlotte Varney. We'll call it four, and Curtis Yates is in the background of all but Rosemary Halkier's, and he may be there yet. Michael Dalkeith was known to be frightened at the time he died – of what or of whom we don't know – but was his death suicide? Did he take us to the grave of Rosemary Halkier, then lie down on top of it waiting for death to take him? But whatever happened, Curtis Yates is in the background there also – he was Dalkeith's landlord and used him for a gofer ... so we believe.'

'So, job sheet time.' Yewdall smiled. 'I sense a job sheet time coming on.'

'It isn't coming on – it's already arrived. So, who's for some action?'

'I'd like a crack at the Dunwoodie murder.' Brunnie sat forwards in his chair.

'I bet you would,' Vicary replied coldly,

168

'but the answer is no. We don't know what the repercussions of your trick with the watering can will be. If A-Ten take the hardest line possible you could be suspended pending disciplinary action.'

'Understood, sir.'

'But apart from that, I want professional detachment, no personal agendas ... allowing that always muddies the water and turns cops into zealots.'

'Yes, sir.'

'So I want you to team up with DC Yewdall – pick up the Rosemary Halkier case from where I left it yesterday afternoon.'

'Very good, sir.'

'The next step there is to interview her best mate who now lives in Mill Hill. She contacted me this morning following my visiting her mother yesterday. She's very happy to talk to us about Rosemary. We need to know what was happening in her life when she disappeared, and especially who the man she was seeing was.'

'So, Swannell and Ainsclough, I want you on J.J. Dunwoodie's murder. That is recent. Very recent. Give it priority, but also dig the case about Charlotte Varney's murder out of the void, press some buttons on that one when you can.'

'Got it, sir.' Ainsclough glanced at Swannell.

'Yewdall.'

'Yes, sir.'

'I'm also putting your name alongside the murder of Gaynor Davies.'

'Yes, sir.'

'We need to know about her, and you'll have to represent the police when her parents view her body. That's a single-hander. But don't go near the address in Kilburn.'

'Of course not, sir.'

'Right.' The phone on Vicary's desk rang and he picked it up. 'DI Vicary.' He paused and listened, and then said, 'Alright, thank you,' and replaced the phone. 'That's A-Ten to see you, Frankie.'

Brunnie nodded.

'They'll just take a statement in the first instance.'

'Yes, sir.'

'After that, pick up the Rosemary Halkier enquiry.'

'Yes, sir.'

'For myself, I am going to read files and pick brains. I want to know all I can about Mr Curtis Yates. Right ... meeting closed.'

Detective Sergeants Swannell and Ainsclough sat in DC Meadows' unmarked car that was parked at the kerb in Kilburn High

170

Road, close to the junction with Messina Avenue, and close to the alley in which J.J. Dunwoodie was beaten to death. It was a cold day with intermittent showers that fell from the low grey cloud which hung over all London. The pedestrians on the greasy pavements huddled in overcoats, and many women had plastic covers over their heads. Occasionally an aircraft was heard, but not seen, flying overhead on its final approach to Heathrow airport.

The police officers sat in a calm, relaxed silence with Meadows in the driving seat, Swannell beside him and Ainsclough in the offside rear seat. A traffic warden approached and tapped on the front nearside window. Swannell wound down the window and, without speaking, showed the traffic warden his ID. The traffic warden nodded and walked on.

'That sort of thing could blow a surveillance operation,' Meadows commented.

'We'd allow for it.' Swannell replaced his ID. 'It just wouldn't happen. We wouldn't park like this, three geezers in a car on a yellow line. Any boy scout could figure us for the law, let alone the nasties.'

'Suppose,' Meadows replied and glanced at his wristwatch, which showed the time to be mid-morning. 'She'll be arriving any

171

time now; she'll be wanting her breakfast. The supermarket took all the sell-by date expired stuff off the shelves last thing before they closed, and they take it to the skip mid-morning. So that's when they arrive.'

'They?'

'The skip-divers ... like these three.' Meadows indicated three pale, sickly, ill-clad youths weaving through the foot passengers and making their way to the alley. 'Early birds,' he explained, 'out to get the worm. It might help them, it might not.'

'No?'

'Well, they don't look hard enough to fight their corner ... three delicate waifs ... some heavier boys will be able to muscle them aside, especially if they are hungry. But I dare say it's worth taking the shot. You can live out of skips if you have a mind to do so. You can get some nice bits of meat, and salad, fruit ... all still wrapped in cellophane ... nothing wrong with it at all. Eat out of skips, work for cash in hand at night – it makes the dole money liveable on. In India they talk about the "slum dogs" in cities. You don't think we have that here? Not to the same extent or same extreme ... but...' He paused as a red London Transport double-decker whirred and hissed past them, by which time the three youths were standing against a wall taking what shelter they could.

Minutes passed in silence, broken only when Meadows said, 'Here we go...' and Swannell and Ainsclough saw two young men in supermarket smocks carrying armfuls of food from the supermarket towards the alley in which stood the refuse skips. The supermarket workers then stopped by the youths and, looking round nervously, allowed the youths to help themselves to what food they wanted. The youths took food and then melted into the crowd, and the supermarket workers carried on to the alley, carrying what food they still held, and put it into the skip.

'Never seen that before,' Meadows commented, 'taking pity on feral youth. Good for them in a sense but they're dropping the supermarket in the soup, legally speaking.'

'They are?'

'Yes, my understanding is that the supermarket is legally obliged to ensure that all food past its sell-by date is properly disposed of, and that means putting it in a skip. The supermarket is not then liable in the eyes of the law for any food poisoning that might occur if someone then removed the food from the skip, but giving it to hungry people is not disposing of it – that is a public health issue, no matter how charitable it might be and no matter how safe.'

'I see,' Swannell growled.

'Don't know what to do.' Meadows sighed. 'Part of me likes the supermarket employees for doing that, but it's the sack for them if they're seen, and, like I said, there is the public health issue.'

'Quiet word with the supermarket manager,' Ainsclough suggested, 'on the q.t., no names ... possibly just a phone call. Leave it for a day or two so the manager won't be able to identify the workers concerned.'

'Yes.' Meadows half-turned to Ainsclough. 'Yes, I'll do that, that will be the best thing to do. The ferals can still get good food from the skip, they'll just have to scavenge for it and the workers will keep their jobs. Ah ... here she is. See her ... black girl in the green waterproof?'

The officers watched as the girl approached the alley and then, instead of going to the alley and searching the skips as the officers had expected her to do, stood contentedly waiting on the pavement.

'Strange,' Meadows whispered.

'That she isn't skip-diving, you mean?' Swannell watched the girl.

'Yes ... as if ... as if...'

'Anyway, let's pull her, we can't wait all

day.' Swannell made to open the car door.

'No!' Meadows laid a hand on Swannell's arm. 'Let's wait, see what she's doing. My old copper's mind is working now. Appreciate you're investigating a murder but you can afford to wait a minute or two.'

'A scam?' Ainsclough commented from the rear seat.

'Possibly. Those two supermarket workers may not be so charitable after all.'

The three officers continued to sit in the car, and then soon after the black girl had positioned herself at the entrance to the alley the same two supermarket workers appeared – two young men; one with distinct fiery red hair, the other overweight and prematurely balding, but both carrying boxes of food. When the two workers reached the girl, the red-headed one stopped and handed her the food, whilst the other carried on and put the food he was carrying into the skip.

'Dare say something has to be seen to be thrown away.' Meadows spoke softly as the girl put the food into a hemp shopping bag and then walked, conveniently, towards the car in which the officers sat. As she approached, Swannell got out of the car, grabbed the girl by the arm and showed her his ID. He opened the rear door of the car and bundled her on to the back seat next to Ainsclough. The girl tried to open the car door but could not do so.

'Childproof locks,' Meadows explained as Swannell sat in the front passenger seat. 'Been shopping, darling?'

The girl glanced at the shopping bag. 'It's all out of date. You can check.'

'We will,' Meadows replied. 'Nice bit of meat you have there ... leg of lamb ... very nice.' He turned and sifted through the contents: steak, bacon, milk, cheese...

'It's all out of date, so why lift me? The boys in the supermarket just help us out, saves us from having to poke around the skip...'

'You saw a geezer getting tanked a few nights ago.'

'Yeah.'

'Well, we want to talk to you about that.'

'Oh.' The girl relaxed. 'I already told them everything.'

'Possibly, we need to go over a few details,' Swannell explained.

Meadows started the car.

'Where we going?'

'Kilburn nick,' Meadows replied.

'It's more comfortable there.' Ainsclough reached over and picked up an item of food from the shopping bag, and read the sell-by date. 'Ah ... you have a time machine, I see.'

'Meaning?'

'Meaning this packet of lovely Danish bacon, smoked back, won't reach its sell-by date until the day after tomorrow. Meaning you're either forty-eight hours ahead of the rest of the world or you have just received a bag load of stolen gear.'

'So, my old copper's mind was right.' Meadows pulled into the traffic lane. 'Neat, this will help my conviction rate; it's been a bit low of late.'

'Quite a nice little earner you have here.' Ainsclough continued to examine the contents of the bag.

'I don't get to keep it all.' The girl sighed. 'I just have to keep it for the evening. I'll likely get to keep the bacon, the milk and the bread but that's all. Just to keep me going. Most times I dip and dive the skips.'

'Who takes the rest?'

'Not saying.'

'It's the old song that's playing. You know, that music echoing in your ears; the tune that you've heard somewhere before.'

'I don't hear no music.' She glanced angrily out of the window.

'Course you do, darling,' Meadows replied. 'It's that old singalong favourite, "You can work for yourself or you can work against yourself" – that song. Have you got anything hanging over you?'

'Three months suspended for two years – got that about six months ago ... shoplifting. I've been inside. I don't like it.'

'Well, you're going back for another three months, as well as anything you get for receiving stolen goods.'

The girl leant forwards, covering her face with her hands.

'That's if we charge you,' Swannell said. 'We have the discretion to charge you or not.'

'Really!' The girl looked up. She was frail and finely made.

'Yes, really; it all depends on how much you help us,' Meadows replied. 'There's two investigations now. I'm a local copper, Kilburn is my manor. I want information from you about the scam going down at the supermarket. I don't need to give your name, you just give me the names of the geezers involved and let me know when the supermarket staff are going to be walking down the street with valid ... food that isn't past its sell-by date. Get to feel their collars when they're off the premises and they're in the bucket.'

'Yeah?' The girl became excited.

'Yeah,' Meadows replied, 'and these

gentlemen are from New Scotland Yard. They want to know about the assault you witnessed the other night.'

'We want details,' Swannell growled. 'Hold anything back about either investigation and you're going inside.'

'So do some thinking between now and Kilburn nick,' Ainsclough added. 'You know, nice crystal-clear thinking.'

Harry Vicary stood and smiled as Garrick Forbes entered his office. The two men shook hands warmly.

'A-Ten never gets this kind of greeting.' Forbes returned the smile. 'So refreshing.'

'Yes, but you and I go back. I did wonder if it might be you when they told me that A-Ten was here. Do take a pew. Coffee? Tea?'

'Tea for me, please.' Garrick Forbes, large and occasionally jovial, but always serious-minded when he needed to be, sat in one of the vacant chairs in front of Vicary's desk. 'Never was much of a coffee wallah ... and speaking of liquid refreshment, we never did have that beer we promised ourselves. It's not often you look down the barrel of a gun, even as a copper.'

'It isn't, is it?' Vicary turned to the table in the corner of his office, on which stood a kettle and a bag of tea bags, powdered milk and an assortment of half-pint mugs. He checked that the kettle had sufficient water and then switched it on. 'Have you been back there?'

'Twice … last autumn.'

'Me too, also twice. I'll go again, not now though–' he pointed to the window – 'hardly the weather for it, but I understand that what we are doing is called "trauma bonding".'

'Really?'

'If you have been traumatized at a specific location you are bonded to that location, and by visiting it, you begin to aid the process of adjustment. So, the people who escaped the King's Cross fire all those years ago still visit the underground railway station … they are drawn to it, but with decreasing frequency as the adjustment progresses, and in the States, folk who escaped the Twin Towers in 2001 visit Ground Zero, but similarly with decreasing frequency as the years pass.'

'Trauma bonding.' Forbes pursed his lips. 'I'll remember that.'

'We should visit together, then have that beer – there's a couple of good interesting pubs in and around Northaw village.'

'Yes, we'll do that, it would be cathartic.' He took the mug from Vicary's hand and mumbled his thanks. 'Doing some heavy reading, I see.' He indicated the files on Vicary's desk.

'Yes ... yes ... and in more ways than one.' Vicary slid behind his desk and resumed his seat. 'Heavy in the sense that it is a thick file – a lot to get through – but also heavy in the sense of its content. It's the file on a felon called Curtis Yates ... apparently he kept a tiger.'

'A tiger!'

'So it is alleged, but they are not easy to acquire, so I don't know how much credence to give to that story ... allegedly used the beast as an "enforcer".'

'Oh ... but you say allegedly.'

'Yes, I don't know what to believe – some of the things in here are quite extreme but are only allegations.' He tapped the file with his palm. 'But the accumulation of unsupported reports does begin to sway one after a while.'

'Yes, I know what you mean; it's like that in A-Ten, building a case against corrupt coppers is like walking in thick smoke looking for flames.'

'I can imagine, but this geezer is one slippery customer. We are interested in the murder of three people known to have some association with him, and he might have driven another to take his own life, and, reading his file, two previous lovers and his wife disappeared. The geezer just does not keep his friends for very long.'

'Blimey, I see the reason for your suspicions. See them clearly. Has he done time?'

'Yes, he pleaded not guilty to murder but guilty of manslaughter, and the CPS accepted the plea. He was out in five years, so we have his dabs and DNA on file, and sufficient evidence for him to do his rite of passage number to gain the street cred he needed ... but nailing him will be a struggle – he uses gofers for all his dirty work and he holds a terror for some people.'

'Any visible means of support?'

'A property company in Kilburn renovating run down properties and renting them to high-end tenants.'

'Very useful if you want someone to disappear ... all those cellars ... all that concrete.'

'Yes, that observation has been made. He also has an import/export business in the East End. Those are two that we know of, and go to provide him with a house in Virginia Water.'

'Not bad.'

'Indeed. I do wonder what naughties the import/export business conceals.'

'Drugs ... illegal immigrants?'

'Yes, my thinking also – not expressed yet – but those are the lines I am thinking along. So, you have had a chat with Frankie Brunnie?'

'Yes, and the upshot is that we won't be instigating disciplinary action against him.'

'Good. I am relieved.'

'He is consumed with guilt over the death of the office manager.'

'J.J. Dunwoodie?'

'Yes, that's the man, but that is not the reason we are not proceeding against him. What clears him is that the office manager permitted him to remove the watering can, even though Brunnie might well have coerced him into doing so without the ability to foresee the consequences. The fact remains that the watering can was nevertheless removed with the consent of the office manager. We have taken a statement from him but we still have to take a corroborative statement from a ... DC Yewdall.'

'Penny Yewdall, yes.'

'The practice of obtaining fingerprints like that is widespread anyway – did it myself once or twice. Can't use prints obtained like that to prosecute, but it's very useful to know who you're dealing with.'

'Yes ... yes ... and Brunnie has helped this

case enormously, and I understand the guilt you mention. Frankie Brunnie is a very ethical, steadfast human being. I have always found him to be a gentleman.'

'Good. Well, just the interview with DC Yewdall and we'll wrap it up.' Garrick Forbes stood.

'Oh ... I visited Archie Dew's widow.' Vicary also stood.

'How is she?'

'Bearing up but feeling the loss, and her daughter is still in residential psychiatric care.'

'Wretched woman, must be difficult for her ... He was so near retirement and that little toerag who shot him will be on the outside soon.'

The two men shook hands. 'I'll phone you in the spring; we'll take that trip out to Northaw Great Wood, then have that beer.'

'Yes, please do,' Forbes turned to go. 'I'll look forward to that.'

'Mr Vicary?' The woman opened the door of her house on Oakhampton Road, Mill Hill. She had short hair and a ready smile, and had worn well with age; even though she was in her early middle years, Frankie Brunnie thought she still looked fetching in tee shirt, jeans and sports shoes.

184

'No.' Brunnie held up his ID. 'I am DC Brunnie, this lady is my colleague, DC Yewdall, we are calling on behalf of Mr Vicary. He is our senior officer.'

'Ah, I see. Pleased to meet you anyway. Do please come in.'

The two officers stepped over the threshold into a warm house – too warm, Penny Yewdall thought, and she did not envy Mrs South her quarterly heating bills – but the warmth within explained why she wore a tee shirt. The house was a neatly kept, 1930s semi-detached property, which smelled strongly of furniture polish. Mrs South invited the officers into the rear room of the house, which looked out on to a long, narrow garden and to a cemetery beyond that.

'We are very lucky to be here,' Mrs South announced, 'privileged ... the cemetery beyond the garden and the golf club at the end of the road; lots of open space; fairly clean air considering that this is the middle of north London. Do sit down.' Mrs South indicated the vacant chairs and settee with a very, Brunnie thought, French-style flourish of her hand. 'My mother phoned me,' she said as she and the officers sat in the armchairs. 'It is about Rosemary Halkier...'

'Yes. You are Mrs South ... once Miss North?'

'Yes.' The woman grinned sheepishly. 'It always causes comments to be made. I was Pauline North from Leyton, I am now Pauline South from Mill Hill ... gone northwards to become South. The jokes are endless. I went to Sussex University and married one of my tutors; he was a junior lecturer then. He's now a professor at Royal Holloway. I teach children now my own are up and away ... no regular post, I am a supply teacher – explains why I am home today ... no phone call from the agency.'

'It seems you have done very well.' Penny Yewdall smiled.

'Yes.' Pauline South nodded briefly. 'I am very fortunate ... successful husband, two lovely boys ... good marriage. I am fulfilled but Rosemary should have had the same. Was it really her on Hampstead Heath?'

'Yes,' Brunnie replied, 'I am afraid it was.'

'Oh ... and I have all this – still alive and all this – but I appreciate it. I appreciate each day because I know that tragedy can strike at any time; you just have to open the newspaper and read about a tragedy striking some poor family.'

'That's a good attitude to have.'

'It's the only attitude. So, how can I help you? I knew that something had happened to her.'

'Oh?'

'Well, I mean, no details, just that some ill must have befallen her ... some misadventure. Like the fell walker who vanished up in the Lake District and three or four years later his body was found in a mountain stream. The search party swept the wrong area for some reason, and then years later another walker attempted to cross the stream at the same location and so found the body – just ten feet either side and he would have missed the corpse. But that wasn't Rose, she wasn't adventurous like that ... but she wouldn't walk out on her life and reinvent herself. That's something that people could do up until the end of the Second World War, but now our National Insurance number and health records follow us everywhere ... all on computer. So really that just left foul play to explain what happened to her ... but she was bright at school, she could have, should have, gone on to university, but she married a fairground worker. Can you believe that? And her life never recovered. Some mistake.'

'So, tell us about Rosemary, if you can,' Brunnie said, 'we are trying to piece together her life at about the time she disappeared.'

'Well, I was at university, but at home ...

must have been between terms, and I well remember her dad coming to our door asking if we knew where she was. Poor soul, he was in a terrible state.'

'What do you know about her social life at the time?'

'Not much. We went out for a drink occasionally, just two Leyton girls together ... up the boozer, like good local girls. The landlord of the Coach and Horses knew us, as did the locals, and he and the locals would not let anyone bother us. We just had a couple of glasses of wine and a right good chit-chat ... but we were drifting apart by then, and we never went up town together.'

'Understood.'

'Any man friend? Rosemary's man friend, I mean.'

'Just one ... and not a good one.'

'Oh?'

'Yes. Strange name...' she took a deep breath. 'How embarrassing, so strange that I have forgotten it.' She forced a smile. 'It'll come ... it'll come, the name is that of the American film star, except his surname is that of the first name of her boyfriend at the time. What was it? What was it? Oh ... Curtis, that's it. Tony Curtis was the actor and Curtis something was Rosemary's boyfriend.'

'That's very interesting.' Brunnie turned to Yewdall, who raised an eyebrow.

'Is it?' Pauline South asked.

'Yes, it dovetails neatly, very neatly into other information we have.'

'I see.'

'So what did she tell you about Curtis X?'

'Curtis X, I like that. Curtis X ... well, she was not comfortable with him; he seemed to have betrayed her and she seemed frightened of him.'

'Betrayed her?'

'Perhaps that is the wrong word. Not so much betrayed as deceived her. It was a case of the old, old story of the man who could charm the birds down from the trees and then once ensnared, turns out to be a monster of a person who destroys all and everything he comes into contact with. And she fell for his charms, possibly as a reaction to the fairground worker she had married and who she was escaping from – that made her even more vulnerable to Curtis X's charms.'

'Oh...' Penny Yewdall groaned.

'You've met the type?' Pauline South asked.

'Oh yes ... often, all too often – not personally but in police work. We have met the victims ... either dead or alive, the victims of the easy charms of the predatory psycho-

189

paths who can smile as they kill.'

'I don't know exactly how they met but I think it was in some dimly lit pickup parlour in the West End, or maybe it was the East End – an East End nightclub. She did say he was an East Ender, like she was, so they had that in common, and he was good looking, and also charming, as you have said. I think they became an item quite quickly. She was easy pickings for him. It got sour though, got sour very rapidly.'

'Oh?'

'Yes, she came home with a bruised face, and after a stupidly short period she went back to him, though she never actually moved in as such. She wouldn't leave her children but was with him every weekend. I do remember her telling me that he had some strange hold over her. She said she knew that she shouldn't go back to him, that he was bad news, but she still felt the tug to return to him in his huge house in Surrey.'

'Surrey?' Brunnie repeated. 'Large county...'

'Virginia Water, she mentioned Virginia Water. The houses down there, like palaces she said, but she felt this magnetic draw to Curtis, which she said she knew she had to resist but she couldn't resist at all.' Pauline South paused. 'It was as though he had

190

some form of control over her.'

'Yes, I know what you mean. It's not untypical with that sort of personality. If the victim is weak enough or needy enough that manner of control can be exercised.'

'Interesting, frightening also, but she was a lovely girl, very attractive. We made an odd couple in the Coach and Horses: me short and plain and she the glamorous, raven-haired, Rubenesque beauty, but inside she was so full of unmet need. She felt really guilty.'

'Guilty?'

'About letting her parents down in respect of her choice of husband ... cheap rented flat in Clacton ... and so the wealth offered by Curtis what's his name was, in her mind, like a compensation, but in fact it was all part of the lure to lead her into the mine-field, so it seems now.'

'You said she seemed frightened?'

'Yes, she had heard that previous girl-friends, or possibly just one girlfriend, had disappeared.'

'How?' Brunnie asked.

'The staff told her.'

'Staff?' Yewdall sought clarification. 'What staff?'

'Domestics ... cleaners ... they clocked her for being an East End girl – their class, not posh; saw her as one of them. She said her name was Tessie ... the cook ... just breakfasts and lunch six days a week. Rosemary told me that Tessie had told her to "get out". Tessie said, "Get out while you're still alive". She returned to her parent's home later that day, and me and her went up to the boozer. That's when she told me what Tessie had said. Then, the next time we met up she told me Tessie had gone. Apparently, she had turned in her notice and walked out.'

'Do you know Tessie's surname?'

'O'Shea.'

'And she lived in Virginia Water?'

'Yes, in some council house development in amongst the mansions, just to balance the social mix and provide cooks and cleaners and gardeners for the hoi polloi.'

'What did she tell you about Curtis X's source of income?'

'A string of businesses, she said, but she also discovered that she had hooked up with a blagger, a serious one, and she suspected that the businesses were there to hide some other activities. She was beginning to wonder what she had gotten herself into – it was about then she vanished.'

Merry Flint scowled at Meadows, Ainsclough and Swannell. 'You can make this go away?'

'We can,' Swannell replied softly, 'if Mr Meadows agrees.'

'I agree. I really want the two supermarket workers who are taking the stuff out. I am not really bothered about the out of work doleys who are taking a meagre slice. It's always better to collar the thieves rather than the receivers. So, yes, I agree.'

'But whether we do make it go away or not is another matter.' Ainsclough also spoke softly. He enjoyed working with Swannell; he had found that both men had a tacit understanding that the whisper is louder than the shout. 'As you told us, Merry, you're under a suspended sentence, so if we charge you then inside you go, you do bird. Again.'

'So it's scratchy backy time?'

'Dare say that's one way of putting it – you scratch our back and we will scratch yours. Help us, we help you. You work for yourself or you work against yourself.'

Merry Flint scowled again. She was, observed Ainsclough, a lighter skinned black girl, possibly of mixed race, but by her loud clothing and beads and bangles she had clearly embraced West Indian culture. However, her speech pattern, apart from the very occasional exclamation, was pure London street-speak. 'So what does the Old Bill need to know?'

'This Old Bill needs to know about the assault the other night, in the alley.' Ainsclough indicated himself and Swannell.

'And this Old Bill wants the S.P. on the supermarket. All of it.'

'So, this Bill first...' Ainsclough leaned forward, 'the other night ... start singing.'

'I was Lee Marvin – hadn't eaten proper for a day or two – so I was skip-divin' in the evening just after it got dark. These two guys turned into the alley. I sat back between the two skips – I was opposite them but they didn't see me ... comes in handy being black sometimes. Thought they was the Old Bill at first – looked the part: tall and fit ... Then I saw they had a little geezer with them, and the little guy went on the deck like about ninety miles an hour. He was clucking ... desperate ... he was pleading, man, pleading so bad. I didn't see no tools, but the two geezers didn't need them, they just stuck the boot in again and again. One bad old kicking he got ... the little guy.'

'Would you recognize them again?' Swannell asked.

'No ... it was dark.' Merry Flint shook her head. 'They were both honkies ... both snowdrops ... tall and fit ... vicious. Don't

194

know how handy they'd be in a level skir-mish, but they don't show no mercy to the little guy, no, man, no mercy ... no mercy at all. He got a slap alright ... no mercy.'

'Beards?'

'No.'

'So they were both clean-shaven?'

'Yes, clean-shaved.'

'Did they say anything?' Ainsclough asked.

'Not a lot.'

'What then? What did you hear?'

'Not much, but I reckoned they belonged to a firm, it wasn't personal to them.'

'Why do you say that?'

'Well, they were kickin' this little guy and then one said, "That's enough ... that'll do", something like that, and the other geezer, he said, "The boss wants it done proper".'

'I see, "the boss"?'

'Yes, so that's what got me thinking that they was part of a firm.'

'Fair enough ... carry on.'

'So the first geezer says, "It's done, he's not getting up", but the second guy just goes on kicking and kicking and kicking ... bouncing the little guy's head off the wall like it was a toy ball.'

'Local accents?'

'Yeah, it was a London team alright, but not posh London; it was Canning Town not

Swiss Cottage.'

'Understood. What else? Anything else you heard?'

'Well, the first one, he just stopped...'

'Stopped?'

'Yes, he was not a happy camper. He helped the other guy put the little guy down, and he put the boot in a few times but the other guy he went at it mental, like ... like he was possessed. It was then that the first guy just stood still. All the time folk was walking past the end of the alley and no one noticed what was going down ... dark and raining. Then the first geezer—'

'The one who was just watching by this time?'

'Yes. He said to the second geezer, "It's done, Rusher. That's it. We need to clear the pitch".'

'"Rusher"?' Swannell repeated. 'He called the second geezer "Rusher"?'

'Yes, I heard it bell-like, "Rusher", that's what he called him. "Rusher".'

'OK, then what?'

'Well, then I suppose Rusher got the first geezer's drift and he stopped putting the wellie in. Then the first geezer, he said, "Let's clear the pitch and get these dugs burned".'

'OK.'

'But you know, I think when he said that he was giving the Rusher character a reason to want to leave, like he had had enough of the aggro and didn't want no more.'

'Interesting.' Swannell tapped his notepad with the tip of his ballpoint.

'So it was like they watch *Crimewatch* on telly and know that the little geezer's blood would be everywhere, so they had to get back to their place, change clothes ... burn the stuff they had been wearing ... burn the old evidence.'

'So they left it at that?' Swannell asked.

'Yeah, they just walked out the alley, calm as you please, like two regular geezers lookin' for a pub on the way home.'

'So what did you do?'

'Legged it, darlin', legged it until I found a phone box, phoned three nines and, like a daft cow, I told 'em my name.' She glanced at the ceiling. 'I mean, how many Merry Flints with form what live in North West Six...? Told 'em what I'd seen and where ... then, like ... soon, like, he was at the door of my flat.' She pointed to Meadows. 'If I hadn't given my name, I wouldn't have been rumbled and pulled. I'm not a grass. I seen what they do to grasses. You know what it means to "cut the grass"?'

'I can guess.'

197

'I heard about a brass that grassed on her pimp ... carried her into the hospital with half her face hanging off, the other half was left lying in the road. So this will make the receiving go away?'

Swannell and Ainsclough glanced at each other. Swannell said, 'Yes, so far as these two Bills from New Scotland Yard are concerned. It can be made to go away.' He and Ainsclough stood.

'But this Old Bill still wants information,' Meadows said, 'so stay put while I escort these two gentlemen out of the nick.'

Merry Flint folded her arms tightly in front of her and stared indignantly at the floor.

Penny Yewdall gently replaced the telephone handset. 'I just love the Welsh accent, so musical.' She smiled across the desks at Frankie Brunnie.

'Isn't it? I know what you mean ... and the least pleasant accent? Birmingham? Yorkshire?'

'Depends what you're at home with, but the Welsh accent ... Anyway, that was the Glamorgan police – Mr and Mrs Davies are travelling to London today to identify their daughter.'

'She has been identified, surely?'

'Yes ... I mean, to view the body. That's what I meant. Help with closure, and they might be able to tell us something – shed a little light – though I hold out little hope.'

'Yes.' Brunnie paused and sat back in his chair, taking his hands slowly from the keyboard, staring with open eyes and mouth at the computer screen. 'Oh my...'

'What!' Penny Yewdall exclaimed. 'What have you found?'

'I'll give you three guesses as to who disappeared at about the same time that Rosemary Halkier disappeared.'

'Not Tessie O'Shea?'

'Yes ... got it in one ... the one and the same. We're getting thin on the ground. We'll have to follow this up, as well as Mrs Pontefract.'

'Well, Mrs Pontefract isn't a suspect, and I can visit her alone.'

'If you could – I can drive to Virginia Water, also alone.'

'I'll let Harry know what we are doing.'

Ainsclough took off his overcoat and hung it on the coat rack, and sat at his desk. He glanced sideways at Penny Yewdall. 'Is Frankie out?'

'Yes.' Yewdall glanced out of the window and smiled as she saw a sliver of blue sky appearing amid the grey cloud. 'Yes, he's just gone to Virginia Water. Well, that is to say he's gone to Sunninghill police station, being the local nick down that neck of the woods, chasing up an old case that might have some bearing on Rosemary Halkier's murder. I am about to go and visit her old workmate, one Miss Pontefract. Hoping I can do that before Mr and Mrs Davies from Pontypool arrive at the London Hospital ... time ... day ... not ... enough.'

'I see.' Ainsclough sat at his desk and logged on at his computer. He tapped the keyboard. 'Rusher', he said absent-mindedly.

'Sorry? As in the Soviet Union, as was?'

'No; mind you, it could be spelled that way. I am assuming it's spelled as in one who dashes about as if in a rush, as in "rush hour". It's a nickname but it's at least a name, and as a nickname it's a damn sight more useful than a "Nobby" or a "Charlie".'

'Yes ... I once ran a felon to ground by chasing his street name of "Dogheaver", not many "Dogheavers" in London. Well none now, he collected life and is in Durham E Wing.'

'A hit ... a hit ... a palpable hit...' Ainsclough clenched his fists at shoulder height. 'I think there is no need to check the spelling, R-u-s-h-e-r seems correct. One "Rusher" aka Oliver Boyd, thirty-one years ... form for GBH, assault with a deadly weapon ... dishonourable discharge from the army for organizing a post office robbery. We need this man in the quiz room ... need his mate also.'

'Oh?'

'Yes, Oliver "Rusher" Boyd sounded to be the real hard case, he did most of the work in J.J. Dunwoodie's murder. His oppo seemed to want him to ease up.'

'Try known associates,' Yewdall suggested.

Ainsclough tapped the keyboard. 'Just one,' he announced, 'a geezer called Clive Sherwin, aka "The Pox".'

'"The Pox"?' Yewdall smiled.

'Yes, doubt you'd call him "The Pox" to his face, but yes. Let's look at him.' He continued to tap the keyboard, 'Yes, he's well known: GBH, handling stolen goods, driving offences ... one short stretch in the slammer. You know it's really only the Grievous Bodily Harm that puts him in the same league as Rusher – seems a much gentler guy really, all in all. You know if it was Sherwin in the alley with Rusher that night, he's the one to lean on, not Rusher, that will be a two-hander.' He paused. 'Me and Swannell it seems...'

'Seems ... unless you hang fire.' Yewdall stood. 'I have to go out.'

Penny Yewdall signed out and drove out to Barking, and then to Bower House, off Whiting Road. The address revealed itself to be a complex of medium-rise inter-war council developments; clearly part of the 'Homes fit for Heroes' movement after the war to end all wars. Rachel Pontefract lived on the third floor of the furthest block of the Bower House Estate. She was short, had a round face, steely eyes, and was not keen to have Penny Yewdall in her home. The interview was thusly conducted with Rachel Pontefract standing on the threshold of her flat and Penny Yewdall standing on the windswept outer landing.

'Can't really tell you much. Yeah, me and Rose did have a few nights out together but I didn't know her well at all.'

'What did she say about her boyfriend at the time she disappeared?'

'Just she wanted away from him but couldn't find the old door marked "exit".'

'I see.'

'She was a good girl and she'd found that her man was a blagger, that he'd done time, and folk who got in his way tended to perform the old vanishing act.'

'Is that what she told you?'

202

'Not using those words darlin' but you know, the gist is still the same. She was a good girl who had just found out her man was well out of order and known to the Old Bill. In the early days she thought he was as sweet as a nut; by a few weeks in she was not well impressed no more. She said she must have been a right pillock to have got so far in. She said she had to get out or she was certain to get bumped ... take the short cut out the door through a high window ... or maybe just vanish ... but she couldn't see no old door with "exit" in big red letters on it – no, she couldn't – and it all started because he had a fancy jam jar ... Rolls Royce, Bentley, Merc ... it meant something to her that did after she walked out on her last old man who could provide nothing but a damp little place in Clacton. Swapping dodgems for a Roller, well, that was climbing the right way.'

'Did she mention his name?'

'Curtis. No last name. Just Curtis, me old china, just Curtis.'

Frankie Brunnie sat down in the chair opposite DC Gerrard in the interview suite at Sunninghill police station in Surrey. Brunnie found it a light and airy room, decorated in pastel shades, with armless easy chairs in which to sit round a low coffee table. It was a room designed to make victims of crime relax and speak as freely as possible, rather than to interrogate suspects. It also clearly doubled as a room in which visiting officers could be welcomed and accommodated. Brunnie glanced out of the window as a sudden but short rainfall splattered on the pane and saw a small stand of cedars swaying in the zephyr. 'Winter's not giving in without a fight,' he commented.

'Seems so.' Gerrard too glanced out of the window. 'But in fairness, this isn't bad for January, too early to expect spring yet.'

'Yes, reckon I'm impatient.' He turned to Gerrard who seemed to Brunnie to be elderly for a detective constable, a man who most probably had just not made the grade when his grey hair was black. 'So, Mrs O'Shea?'

'Yes, I have the file here,' Gerrard patted a manila folder, 'foul play.'

'You think?'

'Well, just take a squint at the profile ... fifty-five years old, comfortably married ... children off her hands ... six grandchildren to rejoice in – just a gentle soul who lived in a council house on the edge of Virginia Water. The sort of person who would likely describe herself as "just a simple person". If folk like that are reported missing they very rapidly turn up, or their corpse is very soon found – they do not remain missing for ten years. Not in densely populated north Surrey.'

'Rather suspect you're right.'

Gerrard scanned the missing persons report. 'Went to work as usual, humbly cycling on her old black bike, and just did not return home that afternoon. Her employer said she left at the usual time, about half past midday, having prepared the food for lunch and left it on a hotplate. So why is New Scotland Yard interested in her?'

'We are ... well ... how to put this ... we are more interested in her employer, Curtis Yates, who is using the name Pilcher.'

Gerrard's jaw dropped. 'Pilcher is Curtis Yates!'

'You know the name?'

'Do I know the name? Do I know the name? He's a real villain, the Drug Squad have been interested in him for a long time. My brother is a detective sergeant there. He has mentioned that name a few times ... fly ... and slippery. We never had cause to suspect him.' Gerrard glanced at the file. 'You see, he gave his name as Pilcher and it was a mis per enquiry. All we can do is take statements until the person or the body turns up.'

'Of course.'

'Well, well ... so now we know where he lives. That's been a puzzle for a while. He has an accommodation address but he does not live there.'

'We are interested in talking to him about a number of folk who go missing or are murdered in his orbit of influence.'

'Including a middle-aged cook?'

'Including a middle-aged cook.' Brunnie stood. 'I'll go and pay a call on her husband, if he is still with us. He'll be late-sixties now, possibly older. I'll also let my governor know of the Drug Squad interest in Yates.'

'I'll phone my brother—'

'No!' Brunnie said sharply, sensing then why Gerrard had not risen in the police force. 'We must keep the communication within official lines.'

'Mrs Davies?' The woman was much older than Yewdall had anticipated. She was also alone, and not, as Yewdell had expected, accompanied by her husband. She hoped the shock did not show on her face.

The woman stood. 'No, I am Mrs Owen – Gaynor's grandmother and her closest relative.'

'I see, thank you for coming.'

206

'Her mother is in Jamaica. She went off with a West Indian seaman she met in the docklands of Cardiff. She left Gaynor with me ... just dumped her on me. I did my best, I wanted to be a tidy parent but she was a difficult girl.' Mrs Owen was short and frail, with curly silver hair. 'You know she would sit on the kerb looking lost and forlorn, telling the neighbours I wasn't feeding her, and I would have my lifelong friends hammering on my door telling me to feed Gaynor. It's like that in Quakers Yard you see, everyone knows everyone else and their business. Eventually the Social Services took her into care because she was stealing from shops – out of my control. Well, if your mother dumps you on your granny when you are just five years old what can you expect? First they tried to foster her with younger adults but that didn't work out. Eventually she went to live in a specialist children's home in Pontypool. Then she ran away to London.'

'Any contact?'

'A postcard or two and a letter – she said she was working for the "big man" with a big house in the south of London, but Gaynor, you could never believe anything she told you.'

'Did she mention a name?'

'Just the location of the house. It was like an American state. It has slipped my mind...'

'Virginia Water?'

'Yes.' Mrs Owen smiled. 'Yes, that was it, Virginia Water.'

'So ... shall we view the body?'

'Yes.' Mrs Owen took a deep breath. 'Yes, it is what I came for. I won't believe it unless I see her for myself.'

'It won't be like you might have seen on television. You'll be separated by a pane of glass, a large pane of glass.'

'I see.'

'She'll be tightly bandaged with just her face visible and it will appear that she is floating in space, floating in blackness.'

'That sounds very sensitive.'

'It is – it's very clever the way it's done. Shall we go?'

Mr O'Shea was tall but frail, with liver-spotted hands and face. His house smelled musty and was cluttered with inexpensive items collected by him and his wife over the years, so it appeared to Brunnie – mainly souvenirs from southern holiday resorts like Margate, Southend-on-Sea, Brighton and Ramsgate. 'She was a worried woman.'

'Worried?'

'Seemed frightened but she felt she had to

go to work to bring in the money. I'd just retired with no pension to speak of. I told her we could manage on the State Benefits but she wanted that extra bit to be able to buy the grandchildren something on their birthdays and at Christmas. So off she'd cycle each weekday morning.'

'Did she say what she was frightened of?'

'No, but once she was more edgy than usual and she said, "She's worse than he is and no mistake".'

'She?'

'Yes ... definitely. "She's worse than he is."'

FIVE

Harry Vicary turned off Commercial Road and drove down a narrow side street of mainly, but not wholly, Victorian era buildings and the easily located Continental Removals. The sign was loud – black writing on a yellow background – and evidently kept clean of East End grime. The premises of Continental Imports/Exports revealed itself to be a large yard set back from the road, a garage beyond that capable of accommodating three high-sided removal vans. It was surrounded on three sides by high, soot-blackened brick walls. To the left of the yard was a green-painted garden shed which evidently served as an office. Two men wearing overalls stood beside the shed and eyed Vicary with hostility as he left his car and walked towards them. 'Morning,' Vicary said cheerfully.

'Get lost, mate,' replied the taller of the two men. 'Go on, sling it ... vanish.'

'Can't do that.' Vicary showed his ID.

210

The shorter of the two men said, 'I'll go and get the boss,' and turned away, walking towards the door of the shed.

Vicary put his ID back in his jacket pocket. 'Now tell me, why on earth would your friend want to do that?'

'Do what?'

'Go and get his governor – strange re-action for someone to have the instant they see a police officer's warrant card, don't you think?'

The taller of the two men glanced at the other man and glared at him as if to say 'idiot'.

And that, Vicary thought, really makes me suspicious but he said, 'So this is part of Curtis Yates's little empire, I believe?'

'Maybe,' the tall man growled.

Vicary saw a slender, middle-aged woman emerge from the shed, followed by an equally slender woman in her early twenties; both had hard faces and cold eyes, and could have been mother and daughter, though Vicary doubted that that would prove to be the case. Fathers and sons in mutual villainy ... but mothers and daugh-ters ... rare, very rare in his experience.

'The Bill?' the older woman asked.

'Yes, making enquiries about Curtis Yates.'

'Why?' Her voice was hard-edged.

'We believe he might be able to help us in our enquiries. We understand he has the property rental business in Kilburn and this business–' Vicary pointed to the yard – 'importing and exporting to Europe, and they provide an income sufficient to support a large house in Surrey. What goes to Europe and what comes back from Europe?'

'This is a legitimate business!' The younger woman snapped. 'Kosher.'

'And you are?'

'Felicity Skidmore.'

'Ah ... now that name rings bells. Didn't you look after the office in Kilburn after Mr Dunwoodie was attacked and murdered?'

'Yes, just two days; got another manager there now. I'm an East End girl, I don't like going out of the East End. We don't travel well 'cos we've already arrived. How do you know I was there anyway?'

'My officers visited. I read their recording.'

'Oh, you write everything down?'

'Everything. I'll be writing this down.' He turned to the older woman. 'You'll be the governor?'

'Yes.'

'Your name, please.'

'Gail Bowler.'

'You must have known Mr Dunwoodie?'

'Yes, wrong place at the wrong time. It happens.'

'You think?'

'What other explanation is there?'

'That he was targeted. You see, it was following up the leads in the Dunwoodie murder that we found out that Mr Pilcher, is also known as Curtis Yates ... interesting why he should use an alias ... and the witness—'

'Witness!' Gail Bowler sounded alarmed. 'You have a witness to Dunwoodie's murder?'

'Yes. A very good one – gave a very good description of Mr Dunwoodie's attacker. In fact, since I am here, I wonder if you could look at the E-FIT we have compiled based on the witness testimony.' Vicary took a brown envelope from his inside jacket pocket, and from it he extracted a glossy E-FIT showing a bald-headed, moon-faced man which he handed to Gail Bowler. She took it and smiled. 'No, I don't know him.'

'We think he's about twenty years of age – a youth, high on drugs maybe, or someone sent to attack Dunwoodie.'

'Well, I don't recognize him.'

'How about you, Miss Skidmore?'

Felicity Skidmore took the E-FIT and glanced at it. 'Nope.' Though she too show-

213

ed some amusement, or some relief, at the sight of the E-FIT. She handed it to Vicary.

'Gentlemen.' Vicary handed the E-FIT to the two overall-clad men, who both seemed anxious to look at it, and again, both held it, looked at it and smiled as they viewed it.

'Sorry, squire.' The taller of the two men handed the E-FIT back to Vicary. 'No recognition.'

'Thank you anyway.' Vicary slid the E-FIT back into the envelope. 'We'll ask around Kilburn, but since I was here I thought I'd take the opportunity ... just on the off chance.'

'So, just the one geezer attacked Dunwoodie?' Gail Bowler said, smart in a grey suit.

'According to the witness.'

'He wasn't a big man.' Gail Bowler spoke with a marked degree of satisfaction. 'He couldn't have put up much of a fight. One man could easily have done it.'

'Seems so.' Vicary paused. 'So this is part of Yates's empire?'

'Possibly.' Bowler again became defensive. 'I see.'

'Vicary? You said your name was Vicary?'

'Yes, Detective Inspector, New Scotland Yard, Murder and Serious Crime Squad. Do tell Mr Yates I was asking after him.'

'We will, don't worry.'

'How long have you been working for Mr Yates?'

'A little while,' Bowler replied.

Vicary glanced across at the two men and then at Felicity Skidmore. 'Same,' the tall man said, 'a little while.'

'Well, do be careful.'

'Careful? Why?' Gail Bowler asked with a note of fear in her voice.

'Because,' Vicary replied, 'because, you see, people who move in his circle ... how shall I put this? They tend to disappear ... or get murdered.'

'You don't say.'

'I do say. You see, the gofer of Mr Yates, Michael Dalkeith by name – strange story. You know he actually lay down in the snow on Hampstead Heath, as though he was committing suicide, but he lay down right on top of a shallow grave which concealed the corpse of a lady called Halkier, Rosemary Halkier, who we believe was romantically involved with Mr Yates when she went missing. It was as though Michael Dalkeith was leading us to her grave, and then at the same time, Mr Curtis Yates's old cook, Mrs O'Shea, went missing ... and Mr Dunwoodie was beaten to death, and he was employed by Mr Yates ... and the Welsh

215

runaway who was found strangled in a room of a house belonging to Mr Yates. So, you see what I mean? He doesn't sound like the man you'd want to take home to meet your parents. Anyway ... I'll say good day.'

Vicary turned and walked back to his car, which stood at an oblique angle to Continental Imports/Exports, and he saw out of the corner of his eye the two men and the two women walk into the garden shed, doubtless to make a phone call. He smiled. He thought he seemed to have put the cat amongst the pigeons quite nicely. 'Just wait and see what springs out of the woodwork now,' he said as he unlocked the door of his car. 'Just wait and see.'

That afternoon Vicary sat with his team in his office in New Scotland Yard; he glanced at Yewdall, Ainsclough, Brunnie and Swannell. 'I took a leaf out of Frankie's book,' he said. 'You don't mind?'

'No, sir, reckon everyone knows anyway.' Frankie Brunnie held up his hands.

'Frankie's method of obtaining Curtis Yates's fingerprints nudged the boundaries of questionable practice, but the upshot is that A-Ten are not taking any action.'

The team members grinned at Brunnie and Penny Yewdall gave him the thumbs-up sign.

'And whether Frankie's actions brought on the murder of J.J. Dunwoodie ... well, we'll probably never know ... and Frankie could not have foreseen the consequences. As I said, I took a bit of a leaf out of his book – out of Frankie's book – and visited Curtis Yates's import and export company in the East End. Four people were there ... one was Felicity Skidmore ... the others I don't know. Anyway, I showed them an E-FIT of a thug we are looking for in an isolated and unconnected case, and told them it was the E-FIT of the person we want to talk to in connection with the Dunwoodie murder. They all looked very pleased when they saw the E-FIT because it clearly didn't look anything like Rusher or Clive "The Pox" Sherwin. So, I think I gave them the clear impression that we were not just barking up the wrong tree, we were in the wrong part of the forest entirely, but more importantly, they were obliging enough to take hold of the E-FIT, each in turn.'

'Fingerprints!' Yewdall said in a hushed but excited tone.

'Yes, which is what I meant when I said that I took a leaf from Frankie's book.' He smiled at Brunnie. 'You put me on the right track there, Frankie. Well...' he tapped sheets of computer printout which lay on his desk. 'The upshot is that all are known to us. Felicity Skidmore has two priors for possession of cannabis ... small fines ... but her prints are on file. The other woman ... I thought she and Felicity Skidmore were a mother and daughter team ... she is one Gail Bowling, though she told me her name was Gail Bowler. Now, she is one very interesting lady, a right madam by the look of her track. She's fifty-three years old, started when she was a teenager ... shop-lifting, receiving stolen goods ... she worked the streets and has convictions for soliciting, then she stopped being a brass and started running them and got five years for living on immoral earnings, which always means she was the top Tom in a brothel – the old brass that runs the younger brasses. Then she did ten years for possession with intent to sup-ply.'

'Ten!'

'Yes ... so a large amount of illicit ... in this case it was Charlie ... a lot of white stuff is why she collected ten years, probably got out in five. So the governor of the import and export business got herself covered in cocaine once. That is significant because Frankie came back from Sunninghill nick with the news that the Drug Squad are interested in Curtis Yates. So I will contact the Drug Squad and let them know of our interest. It might become a joint investigation, but I will insist on having operational command. It's a murder enquiry, possible multiple murders, which takes priority over drug smuggling.'

'Do we know how long Gail Bowling has been associated with Curtis Yates, boss?' Ainsclough asked.

'No. Why do you ask?'

'Because when I visited Mr O'Shea yesterday he mentioned that his wife Tessie had seemed frightened of her employer, or employers, and had made a comment about "she" being worse than "him" or something similar.'

'So, a female accomplice?'

'Yes, sir, possibly, unless the "she" in question is or was no more than an overbearing housekeeper, but I think we need to find out who "she" was … or is.'

'Yes.' Vicary sat back in his chair. 'That's a task. The two men at the yard … one was Rusher, Oliver "Rusher" Boyd, plenty of track for violence – a tall, hard, lean individual. The other was younger, rejoices in the street name of "Mongoose Charlie", Charles McCusker being his real name, twenty-eight years, track for burglary and then he moved up to the league and did time for manslaughter. Sentenced to a five stretch, but probably joined the Christian Union and was drinking IPA again within two years.' He paused. 'So how do we proceed? Curtis Yates is the target but he is well under cover. Seems he's been getting away with too much for too long. People are murdered ... cocaine is possibly imported ... he is probably exporting ecstasy pills, as well, but between us and the Drug Squad we should be able to put a solid case together. Make sure he swaps that large house in Virginia Water for a shared cell in Wandsworth or the Scrubs. His victims deserve justice but Yates doesn't seem to get his paws dirty.' Vicary glanced out of the window of his office as again the rain started to fall.

'We need to find someone who will talk,' Swannell said. 'We would offer witness protection, of course, but it will have to be someone well on the inside, or someone who can provide evidence to link Yates to a murder ... or two.'

'Or perhaps we could insert someone,' Yewdall suggested.

The room fell silent.

Yewdall shrugged. 'Why not? A lassie is less likely to go undercover, and I come from Stoke-on-Trent – I have a genuine Potteries accent if I need to use it ... I'm a proper "Stoker",' she said, pronouncing 'Stoke' as 'Stowk'.

Swannell held eye contact with Vicary. 'It could work, sir. Penny is not known to the staff at WLM Rents ... she could walk in off the streets.'

Vicary turned to Yewdall. 'You'll be in real danger.'

'I know, sir.'

'This will certainly help your career if you do this, but do not let that be your motivation.'

'I know that, sir, and I won't.'

'He'll likely try and make you work King's Cross.'

'I won't agree to that. He'll need to use me as a gofer, if he wants one, which will be more useful to us anyway, I would have thought – carrying parcels from address to address, we could put his network together very well.'

'OK. This will take a week or two to prepare. I'll set the ball rolling. We'll get you into deep cover. But only if you are sure...'

'I'm sure.' Yewdall smiled. 'Very, very sure. I want the king of Kilburn to take a great fall.'

'Good.' Vicary smiled approvingly. 'Meanwhile, let's bring in Clive "The Pox" Sherwin. He sounds a lot softer than "Rusher" Boyd. See what he can tell us.'

'You either like it or you don't,' the ill-shaven man said. 'The thrill is the motivation – it is for me anyway.' He rolled a cigarette, taking the tobacco from a plastic pouch.

'You've been doing this a long time?' Yewdall asked, shivering in a yellow blouse, denim jacket and an old pair of jeans with holes in both knees. She wore an old pair of sports shoes and thin ankle socks.

'Yeah...' he rolled the cigarette painfully thinly, as if it was more paper than tobacco. 'You cold?'

'Yes, but I was advised to get used to it.'

'That's good advice. If you show too much sensitivity to the cold you won't come across as authentic. Do you smoke?'

'No.'

'Well start. Smoke roll-ups like this.' He held up his cigarette.

'I know what roll-ups are.'

'No, I mean roll them like this, as thin as thin can be, that means you've been on the inside. Only a con who is used to trying to make his weekly one ounce ration of weed last a week will roll them as thin as this. It's a good habit to get into. If you are not in the habit, I mean well in, you'll forget yourself and roll a thick one, and your cover is blown.'

'Understood.'

'You'll need to stop washing, maybe just your face now and again, but not a full body wash and don't change your clothes too often.'

'Alright.'

The man lit the cigarette with a blue disposable lighter. 'I am going to be your contact, not your governor. Mr Vicary is it?'

'Yes, Harry Vicary.'

'Met him once, seems to know his stuff.'

'I think he does.'

'I'll give you a phone number which you must memorize and use the continental method.'

'What's that?'

'Break it down into two figure components. For some reason we Brits tend to remember numbers using the individual units, so we would remember a sequence as two, four, seven, eight, six, three, nine, for example.'

'Yes, I would do that.'

'Well, the continentals would remember that number as twenty-four, seventy-eight, sixty-three, nine. Use the continental method, it's easier.'

'Yes, I will.'

'It's a landline.'

'OK.'

'To an address above a travel agents in Finchley.'

'Finchley?'

'Yes.'

'Bit posh.'

'Yes ... posh addresses are very useful, makes it easier to spot nasties hanging around sighting up the joint.'

'Of course.'

'But you won't be going there; the cover address is Lismore Photographic Studios. You can leave a message on the answering machine. We need a code name for you. Did you ever keep a pet?'

'A cat once.'

'What was her name?'

'Spyder, with a "y".'

'Spyder with a "y", that's a good name. It has a certain ring to it. I can remember that.' He drew on the thin cigarette. 'So, you are from the five towns?'

'Yes, Hanley.'

'Your dad still lives there?'

'No, he retired to the coast.'

'Well, he's moved back.'

'He has?'

'Yes, he has. He never left in fact.' The man flicked the ash from his cigarette on to his jeans and rubbed it gently into the weave of the denim with his fingertips. 'Get into habits like this, using your jeans as an ash-tray.'

'OK.' Penny Yewdall glanced around her. The lovingly landscaped grounds of Hither Green Crematorium seemed indeed a perfect place to meet her contact. They seemed to be the only two people in the grounds that were separated from the cemetery by a line of tall poplar trees. They sat on a bench close to the trees on a pathway which formed a U-shape adjoining the main driveway to the crematorium building. SE6 was a long way from Kilburn and a long way from the East End. She had travelled to central London on the suburban overground service, changing trains to ensure she was not being followed. 'You won't be being followed anyway, not on this trip, but it's a good discipline to get into,' was the advice given by the unidentified voice on the phone.

'That's undercover work,' the man who approached her in the grounds had said after they sat down. 'You'll dress like this, you'll be smelly and you'll be uncomfortable, and you'll be looking over your shoulder all the time ... and learn not to stare;

only cops stare. You'll either like it or you won't.'

'I see.'

'It's all for authenticity. Your old man still lives where you grew up, 214 Rutland Street, Hanley, right in the middle of the five towns.'

'Six.' Yewdall smiled. 'There are six towns; Tunstall, Burslem, Hanley, Stoke, Fenton and Longton. It was Arnold Bennett who wrote a book called *Anna of the Five Towns*, which gave rise to the belief that there are five towns in the Potteries.'

'But there's six?'

'Yes.'

'Good. Well, I have learned something, and that sort of thing will help your credibility. The address I gave you exists. You'll be going back to your roots.'

'How did you find out? Why did you choose it?'

'It chose us in a sense. It was up for sale, so we rented it from the outgoing owner for a few weeks. It wasn't selling so it gave him a bit of money. It is his late mother's house so no one is living there. We put some furnishings in ... and your dad is a retired detective sergeant from the Staffordshire constabulary.'

'You don't miss a trick.'

226

'Can't afford to, Curtis Yates is no fool; he won't take you on as even a gofer unless you're fully vetted by his heavies, or his gofers, or his females. You left home some years ago and he won't have a good word to say about you. He'll say, "I don't know where the devil she is ... broke her mother's heart leaving like that"...'

'Wow.'

'Do you have a photograph of yourself about five years old? I mean taken five years ago?'

'I could dig one out.'

'Do so, today. Post it to the Finchley address.'

'The photo studios?'

'Yes. Address it to the manager, and write "Penny" on the rear.'

'I keep my name?'

'Your Christian name, yes. What is your grandmother's name?'

'Which one?'

'Maternal.'

'Smith.'

'Paternal?'

'Lawrence.'

'OK, we'll use that, it's more obscure. Pleased to meet you, Penny Lawrence. We'll get a DSS signing card in that name. Tomorrow you go up to Staffordshire.'

'I do?'

'You do.'

'Walk around the area of your "dad's" house, get to know Rutland Street, the bus routes that service it, the pubs, the schools, the shops.'

'Understood.'

'And polish up your Staffordshire accent. Spend two days up there ... live rough ... buy an old coat from a charity shop, leave all police ID and any jewellery behind in London – carry anything like that and it will be fatal ... and I don't mean fatal ... I mean...'

'You mean fatal. I get the message.'

'Return to the Smoke three days from now and start panhandling in Piccadilly.'

'How will I contact you?'

'I will give you some coins now and also some coins will be given to you by a passing stranger ... he'll be a cop. It's to ensure you have enough money to make a phone call to the photographic studio. You can also write.'

'Write?'

'Why not? Just a postcard with a cryptic message sent to the photographic studio, but it is essential that you write the card and address it the instant before you post it.'

'Yes.'

'Carry around one or two pre-stamped postcards but don't pre-address them.'

'Alright.'

'It's another means of contacting us if all else fails ... but we won't receive the card for twenty-four hours.'

'I realize that.'

'Forty-eight hours if you post it on Saturday.'

'Got you.'

'If you sense that you are in even the slightest danger then come in, find a phone box and dial three nines, or walk into a police station ... or stop a police car or a foot patrol.'

'Alright.'

'Always remember just who it is that you are dealing with.' The man paused as a heavily laden goods train rumbled along the railway line that ran behind the crematorium. 'These people don't need proof beyond a reasonable doubt to off you. All they need is the slightest whiff of suspicion. For them life is cheap anyway, unless it's their own, in which case they all start to scream about their rights.'

'Yes, I've met that type before.'

'Bet you have ... and often. Anyway, here's a couple of hundred quid.' He handed her an envelope. 'Buy a train ticket to Stoke-on-Trent ... go and familiarize yourself with the locality. Remember to get a coat from a charity shop and rough it up, tear a button off and roll it in the gutter a bit.' The man stood, and looked to Penny Yewdall to be every inch an ex-con, a real hard nose; someone you didn't want to give grief to.

'Understood, sir.'

'And get out of police-speak.'

'Sorry, chief, mate, darlin'...'

'Better. Be like a good actor, don't just go through the motion and say the lines, think yourself into the part. Be the character in question, don't pretend to be a young female dosser ... actually become one.'

'Understood.'

'And it starts now. When you get to Hanley, walk round all night, stay up all night, huddle in a doorway if you get really tired.'

'Yes, mate.'

'Get real. Stay out two nights running, get to be that no one wants to sit next to you on the bus or train back to London ... but it's all grist to the mill. Get an early bus or train back ... bus is better, it's cheaper, but get rid of the ticket as soon as. Short of money, coming to London, you'll take the bus.' He handed her a coin-bag containing twenty pence pieces. 'That's for the phone calls to the photographic studio. Keep it separate from any other cash you have. If you're asked about it, say you nipped a geezer for change who was screwing parking meters.'

'If I say that, they'll want me to work King's Cross.'

'So say the geezer was a personal friend, so you didn't sell yourself to a stranger.'

'Good idea.'

'So we'll have to hope Yates will take you as a gofer.'

'Yes, mate.'

The man grinned. 'Don't ask questions. Very important. Remember – be the part, don't pretend, and a dosser who accepts a roof in return for gofering does not ask questions.'

'Got you.'

'Start smoking roll-ups and roll them thin. And look at the ground when you walk down the street.'

'The ground.'

'Yes, scan it, the ground is where you find half-smoked fags and dropped coins, half-eaten sandwiches ... especially round bus stops. If you ask questions and walk looking around you like a cop on the beat, you'll be clocked as an undercover officer and then ... well, then it's goodnight Vienna for you, princess. Frightened?'

'Yes.'

'Good, that'll keep you on your toes. Get

light-fingered, and if you are invited to take part in petty crime, go along with it, and get used to calling the police "pigs", "filth", etc.'

'OK.'

'You won't be staying there long enough to get confused about your identity, which can happen if you stay undercover for long enough.'

'So I have heard. Have you been under long?'

'Don't ask questions,' the man growled.

'Sorry.'

'When you return to London find a pitch in the Dilly Lady subway. I'll find you. Don't show any sign of recognition. Spend any money you collect on food. Find a doss and pick up dirty habits.'

'Like rubbing fag ash into my jeans?'

'Yes, like that ... and use bad language, all you can muster, but let it be natural. People can tell when it's forced.'

'How long do I keep it up?'

'A few days; someone will tell you when to walk into WLM Rents saying that you heard they had drums in return for work.'

'We can't find Rusher – he's gone to ground.'

'He does that,' Clive Sherwin replied casu-

232

ally. 'He plays the mole when he wants to play the mole. If he don't want to be found, he won't be found.' Sherwin glanced to his left at the tape recording machine. The light was off, the spools stationary. 'This is not being recorded?'

'No.' Brunnie smiled. 'This is unofficial, just a casual chat, all nice and cosy.'

'There's nothing cosy about a police station,' Sherwin replied sourly. He was a well-built, muscular man – pleasant, easy on the eye, Brunnie thought; a comfortable six-footer; a man whom women would find attractive, and very tidy indeed ... decorative ... edible in the extreme.

'Dare say that depends upon your situation – you realize you are looking at life if we can convict you of the murder of Dunwoodie?'

'If...' Sherwin sneered.

'We have a witness. How do you think we found you? He heard you address the other geezer as Rusher. A record check – only one felon in the Smoke known as Rusher, and you get flagged up as an associate.'

'So I heard ... that photofit you showed at the removals depot looked nothing like me. Your witness was way off.'

'Oh, that wasn't an E-FIT of you or Rusher, that was just an old E-FIT from an

233

unrelated case – my governor just handed it round to collect a few fingerprints.'

Clive Sherwin's jaw sagged. 'You can do that?'

'Oh yes, we do it all the time, believe me. We can't use any fingerprints gathered in that manner to aid the prosecution's case, but it helps us to let us know who we are dealing with. We like to know who we are up against. E-FITs are useful that way – lovely glossy surface, ideal for gathering finger-prints. Tell me about Gail Bowling.'

'Nothing to tell.'

'She seemed to be in charge of the import/export depot.'

'Did she?'

'Is she linked to Yates in any other way ... other than business?'

'I wouldn't know.'

'You would. You're just not saying. OK, probably safer to say nothing. So what will you tell them?'

'Them?'

'Yates, Bowling, Rusher ... they will know you've been lifted – they'll want to know everything that was said.'

Sherwin looked at Brunnie with wide ap-pealing eyes, like a salesman desperate to make a sale. 'You're in deep, Clive. Very deep. Too deep.'

Sherwin remained silent but Brunnie knew that he had the man's attention.

'You see, Clive ... you don't mind if I call you Clive? You're not a bad lad, not really. OK, so you could be looking at life for the murder of J.J. Dunwoodie, but that doesn't mean you're bad ... not ... evil bad, just easily led. You met Rusher in the army, I believe?'

'Yes. He stood up for me.'

'Did he?'

'Yes.'

'So you feel you owe him?'

'Yes ... there were some heavy boys in the army. A lot of money lending went on, Rusher looked after me.'

'I see ... hence the feeling of owing him something?'

'Yes, reckon you could put it like that ... reckon you could.'

'Or did he just want to put some sense of debt and loyalty into you so you'd be useful to him one day? Geezers do that you know.'

'Do they?'

'Yes ... yes, they do, happens all the time. So did you and Rusher do any more jobs for Yates?'

'This is off the record?'

'It isn't happening at all, my good mate, we are not even here.'

235

'OK, well a few. We got teamed up. We worked well together.'

'With Rusher the wheel man?'

'Wheel man?'

'In the lead.'

'Oh, yes, Rusher always decided what we'd do and how we'd do it.'

'Always you two?'

'No, usually but not always. "Mongoose Charlie" was there as well sometimes, if it was a three-hander. Rusher liked Mongoose because he was handy if you got into a proper skirmish, or if the mark was putting up resistance – but Mongoose and Rusher, they'd argue, and I never argued with Rusher because he knew best.'

'And he'd looked after you when you were in the forces?'

'Yes.'

'We've heard of Mongoose...'

'So why talk to me?'

Brunnie paused. 'Look, Clive...' He glanced up at the opaque panes of glass set high in the walls of the interview room, then down at the orange hessian carpet. 'I'll be straight with you.'

'OK.'

'We are closing in on Yates. We are closing in and we are going to close him down. For good. We have been interested in him for a

236

long time, a lot of summers ... the Murder Squad, the Drug Squad, and we want as many of his lieutenants as we can get as well. He's not hiding behind the likes of Michael Dalkeith any more; he's going to eat porridge, mucho, mucho porridge. He's going down big time.'

'His lieutenants? He's not in the army.'

Brunnie smiled, 'Just an expression. We want his right-hand men, the top fitters.'

'Like "Mongoose Charlie" ... like Gail Bowling, you mean?'

'Yes, like them.'

'I knew it had to come.'

'It had to come?'

'The end.'

'It's been a long time coming, but it's now just round the corner.'

'So soon?'

Brunnie smiled and nodded. 'We can work something out for you.'

'Work something out?'

'You're talking to me. If you carry on talking like this, you could talk yourself into a new life.'

'I heard ... new name?'

'New place to live ... it's called witness protection.'

'Like I said, I've heard of it. They say it doesn't work.'

'Well, they're bound to say that; they don't want you squealing like a stuck pig, telling us where the bodies are buried, but witness protection works. If anyone in witness protection gets chilled, it's always because they blew their own cover. Believe me, it's the real deal ... the full monty ... new identity, new place to live, new National Insurance number, new passport. How old are you now Clive?'

'Thirty-two.'

'Still a youth – time to start again, settle in a new city, forget all this.'

'How far away? I don't want to be too far from London.'

'To be safe, it has to be north of Watford and west of Swindon. We avoid the south coast – too many blaggers take their girls to Brighton for a weekend – you run the risk of being bumped into and then bumped off.'

'Plymouth?'

'Yes, possible ... so's Portsmouth and Southampton, but avoid the holiday resorts.'

'You've set me to thinking.'

'You won't do well in the pokey, Clive. You're a big lad but you're too soft inside. So I am glad I've got you thinking, it's what I intended to do.'

'I'll have to give evidence?'

238

'Possibly.' Brunnie opened his right hand. 'But if you tell us where we can find evidence that will convict Yates ... a smoking gun with his prints on it.'

'He doesn't like shooters, too messy, he says.'

'It was just an expression ... just another expression.'

'Yates once told me that only cowboys use shooters – you don't need shooters to off some old geezer.'

'It's really time to start working for yourself, Clive ... help us get Yates off the street, help us seize his assets.'

'Assets?'

'Possessions ... like his house in Virginia Water.'

'He won't be happy about losing that.'

'If he can't prove he bought it with honest cash...' Brunnie shrugged. 'That's what really hurts them – loss of their houses, all the money they've got stashed away. We put the forensic accountants to work under the proceeds of crime legislation ... and they do fifteen to twenty years, and come out to the queue at the Sally Army soup kitchen. That is some drop.'

Sherwin gasped. 'I've seen what happens to grasses. If I grass Yates up, I know what will happen to me. I need to think.'

239

'No worries, think all you like, but if we arrest him without your help, you go down with him ... the clock's ticking, Clive. If you want to turn Queen's evidence, all you need to do is to walk into a police station, any police station.'

'They watch police stations. They'll have seen me being brought in.'

'So take a train to somewhere outside the smoke.'

'I need to think.'

'So think, Clive. I'd like to say take your time, but I can't ... because you can't.'

Penny Yewdall had survived for forty-eight hours, and sat on the steps of the underground at Piccadilly Circus with a small white plastic beaker resting on the ground in front of her. An occasional coin was dropped therein, but for the most part, almost the whole part, people passed her in their hundreds, if not thousands, and spared her not a glance. She slept in doorways and spent what money she had on fast food from street vendors. On the morning of the third day she walked from Piccadilly Circus to Kilburn and entered the premises of WLM Rents. She approached the man at the desk hesitantly; she felt unkempt, unwashed. 'Posh in here,' she said looking about her.

'Too posh for you, darling.' The man in his thirties behind the desk avoided eye contact.

'Well they say out there that you have rooms for dossers ... just askin'...'

The man sat back in his chair and looked at her. He had a hard face, the face of an ex-con. If he did posses a sense of humour, Yewdall felt that it must live deep within his psyche.

'Is that what is said?'

'Yes.'

'Word gets round.' He paused. 'What else is said?'

'That it's not free. You have to work.'

The hard man gave a very slight nod of his head. 'How old are you?'

'Old enough.'

'That's not what I asked.'

'Twenty-four ... but I'm not working the street. Not for anything, not for anyone.'

'What's the accent?'

'Potteries ... Stoke-on-Trent way.'

'Got a name and an address up there?'

'Penelope Lawrence, Two-one-four Rutland Street, Hanley.'

'I'll make a phone call. Come back in a couple of days Penelope Lawrence, but you will have to work. We don't carry passengers.'

'Two days?'

'Two days.' He lowered his head and wrote her name and address on his notepad.

The man and the woman sat contentedly side by side in the living room of their house in east London. The man turned to the woman and asked, 'Cocoa?'

Kathleen Vicary smiled. 'Yes, please ... it will help us sleep.'

SIX

The hugely built West Indian male seemed to Penny Yewdall to appear from nowhere, emerging out of the throng that negotiated the steps from Piccadilly Circus underground station to Regent Street. Gold rings adorned his fingers, his shoes were of crocodile skin, and he wore a full-length leather coat with an expensive looking suit beneath it. He towered over her and she caught a powerful scent of aftershave. They made eye contact. 'Pretty chick,' he sneered.

Penny Yewdall ignored him and glanced away.

'Pretty chick, pretty white chick ... pretty honky chick ... little snowdrop chick. Come with me girl, I can show you how to make some real money ... real bread.'

She still ignored him.

'Real soft bed, chick ... warm bed, clean sheets, better than this cold and damp stairway, pretty chick.' The man's harassment of her was public, naked, yet not one person intervened on her behalf. 'Good clothes, new clothes.'

She continued to ignore him.

'Real money, chick,' he chanted, 'jewellery, good clothes.' Then he bent further towards her, hinging at the waist with powerful stomach muscles, so close that Yewdall smelled his minty breath through the fog of aftershave, and then the man said, 'Harry Vicary says to be careful of a geezer called "Mongoose Charlie", he offs people for Yates.' Then he melted away into the crowd, leaving her alone once more, sitting in the drizzle with one or two very low denomination coins of the realm in her little plastic beaker, but comforted by the realization that she was being monitored. The crowd had hidden eyes.

She left the stairs at dusk having developed a strange trance-like detachment from the world, which she realized is the norm for down-and-outs – it was evidently the way they survived, mind and body separated from each other. They spent the days lost in their thoughts and memories and fantasies, and the nights lost in their dreams. Again she ate takeaway food from stalls in the street, curled up in doorways snatching sleep – occasionally she was moved on by a uniformed police officer but somehow survived until she felt it was time to go and sit on the stairs at the 'Dilly Lady' for another day. On the third day, in the forenoon, she walked to Kilburn and entered the premises of WLM Rents.

'I expected you yesterday,' the man said coldly as she approached.

'You said two days.'

'I meant the day after the next day.'

'I thought you meant two full days I had to wait.'

The man sniffed. 'Never mind. We can help you.' He opened a drawer and tossed her two keys on an inexpensive key fob. 'It's 123 Claremont Road. Do you know it?'

Couldn't be better, Yewdall thought, but said, 'No ... I can find it.'

'Left out the door, on the left just before the railway line.'

'Got it.'

'Your room will be the ground floor room, on the left once you are over the threshold.'

'OK.'

'But you'll be working.'

'Not on the street.'

'No. Other jobs.'

'OK.'

Penny Yewdall walked the greasy pavement in a steady drizzle to the address she had been given, the very address central to the investigation, and her room was the room in which the Welsh girl, Gaynor Davies, had been strangled. It could not, she once again thought, it just could not be better. She reached the house and rang the front door-bell. There was no answer. She tried the first key in the lock. It didn't fit and so she let herself in with the second of the two keys. The house was gloomy. Even mid-morning it had a gloom about it and the smell of damp was strong and gripped her chest. 'Hello,' she called. Her voice echoed in the hallway. She walked forward and closed the door behind her, and then let herself into the ground floor room to the left of the hallway. She stepped into the room and stopped. A man stood in the room – tall, muscular, cold eyes. Yewdall and the man stared at each other.

'I was told this was my room,' Yewdall spoke nervously.

'Where you been, girl?'

'None of your business.'

The slap sent Yewdall reeling backwards until she fell against the wall and then to the floor. The urge to retaliate was strong but she resisted it. The handler was correct. She had to role-play, and weakened, emaciated female dossers take the slaps, they don't hit back.

'Where you been!' The man advanced and stood over her, fists clenched. 'Where you been! Where you been!' The man's eyes burned with anger.

'Begging...' Yewdall panted. 'I've been begging.'

'Make any money?'

'Hardly nothing...'

The man pulled her up by her upper arm and threw her against the wall. He felt in her pockets and pulled out a handful of loose change, and the plastic bag containing twenty pence pieces. 'What's this?' He held the bag up to her face.

'Money. It's all I have.'

'Since when do dossers collect twenty pence pieces?' Unlike the large, black police officer, the breath of this man was hot and malodorous, a mixture, it seemed to Yewdall, of gum disease, tobacco and alcohol.

'I nipped a guy for them. He was milking parking meters.'

'You nipped a guy for them but you won't work King's Cross? Mr Yates, he won't like that.' The man gripped her forearm.

'Who's he?'

'The man ... he's the man you work for. You live in his house, then you work for Mr Yates and Gail Bowling – you work for them

247

both.'

'But I knew the guy.' Penny Yewdall turned her head away; she looked down towards the floor. 'Known him for years. We had a thing going once so I didn't see myself as being a brass ... he wasn't a stranger.'

'How does he do it, the parking meters?'

'He uses tweezers – slides them in and the coin pops back out. Filth to worry about and CCTV cameras but he's real quick, real lively.'

'In London?'

'No ... up in Stoke-on-Trent.'

The man sneered and relaxed his grip, but still held her. 'Now I know you're telling the truth – can't do that in London but up in Stoke they're still fighting the Second World War ... primitive. Anyway, get yourself washed and clean your clothes, Mr Yates wants to see you – you'll be working tonight.' He dropped the bag of coins on the floor and let go of Yewdall's arm, then left the room, and went out of the house.

Yewdall stood dazed for a moment, and then collected herself and went to the bathroom, where she stripped and washed herself, and then washed her clothing, rinsing them as much as she could. She wrapped herself in a towel and unlocked the bathroom door. Josie Pinder stood in the hallway. The two women looked at each other.

'I heard you come in,' Pinder said – short, frail, she had to look up at Yewdall. 'Are you OK?'

'Just a slap ... yes ... OK ... I've had worse. He says I'm going to work.'

'Yes, they start you as soon as. That's Sonya's towel...'

'I ... sorry, I don't have one ... I was told to wash.'

'She's out, dry yourself and put it back; I'll tell her I used it.'

'Thanks,' Yewdall mumbled. 'I have clothes that need drying.'

'Bring them to my room; I'll put them over the radiator for you.'

'Good of you.'

'OK, just do as you are told; that way you survive. The last girl in that room, a Welsh girl, teenage runaway, she made good money working King's Cross ... Michael brought her back here.'

'Michael?'

'The guy who had the room, he died on Hampstead Heath ... in the snow. He brought her back one night, bringing her off the street ... rescuing her ... left her here; said he would get her money to send her back to Wales but Rusher and "Mongoose Charlie" came round and strangled her.

They made us watch. Watching someone get strangled...'

'Oh...'

'Well, that was "Mongoose Charlie" just now. They work for Yates. They left the Welsh girl in the room, told us we'd seen nothing, but said if we grassed then that would happen to us.'

'Oh...' Yewdall sank back against the wall.

'Yeah ... right...' Pinder slid past her. 'Bring your kit to my room. That one–' she pointed to the door at the end of the landing – 'you haven't got much there so they won't take long to dry – heater's full on.'

The man closed the curtains of the front room window and sat in the deep armchair and picked up the telephone. He dialled the number which he had been given. 'They've been,' he said when his call was answered. 'Checking up on her, heavy duty boys.'

'Yes, we know. I mean we know they're a heavy team,' the voice replied. 'What did they want?'

'Usual stuff ... what you'd expect ... asking for her. I gave the angry father response ... don't know where she is, she put her mother through hell ... the number agreed, sent her to good schools, Our Lady of Lourdes ... so she brings trouble to the door and runs

250

away, sent us a postcard from London, so that's where she is, London – that's what I said.'

'Good. When was that?'

'Midday.'

'Midday today?'

'Yes. I didn't phone you earlier because I can be seen from the street, and it would have looked suspicious if I had picked up the blower immediately.'

'Yes ... good thinking.'

'They hung about. They waited. Two guys with pinched faces – had wrong 'uns written all over them. I left the house and walked to the shop at the end of the street. One of them followed me so they were checking me out. They just sat in the car smoking fags, yellow BMW, no idea of blending.'

'Bit clumsy for Yates.'

'Well, you'd know that, I wouldn't, but they tipped the contents of their ashtray in the road.'

'Did they indeed?'

'Yes, they did indeed. And it's nice and dry up here. I saw the weather, you have rain in London.'

'Yes, we do, intermittent showers, as they say.'

'Well, dry as a bone here, no threat of rain either. So I'll go out later, much later, walk around – I won't miss a bright yellow BMW – pick up the fag ends; two lovely DNA profiles for you.'

'Thanks. Take care though.'

'Don't worry; it'll be much later though. I'll phone you in the morning when I have them safe.'

'We'll send a motorcycle courier to collect them. Appreciate this.'

'Your old man angry with you, girl?'

'My old ... you mean my dad?' Penny Yewdall sounded alarmed. 'You've seen him?'

'Yes.' The woman had a hard, unforgiving face, Yewdall thought; a menacing tone of voice and cold, penetrating eyes. She reminded Yewdall of Mrs Tyndall – the formidable Mrs Tyndall – head of maths at her school. She had first seen then how true it is that fear is a great learning tool, as when one can recall with great precision the details of an incident in which one nearly lost one's life. Exposed to Mrs Tyndall as she had been, it was, she realized, little wonder that she, and the rest of the form, had made such rapid headway with quadratic equations. But then, and now, she felt sorry for Mrs Tyndall's family. And here was Mrs Tyndall again. Formidable, overbearing, but this time her name was Gail Bowling. Hard as nails, with a lump of granite where all other mortals have a heart. 'Yes, we've met him, we like to know who we have working for us.'

Yewdall allowed a look of fear to cross her eyes.

'But you checked out alright – you would not be standing here if you didn't.'

'That's right,' Curtis Yates added, sitting in the armchair by the log fire, pulling leisurely on a large cigar. 'So we can't make you work the street, but if you want a roof, you need to earn it.'

Yewdall nodded. 'I need a roof.'

'We all do.' Gail Bowling, dressed in a severe black dress and black shoes, handed Yewdall a package. 'Take this.'

Yewdall stepped forward and accepted the package. It was about the size of a paperback book, felt solid, and she thought it quite heavy in proportion to its size. She stepped back, allowing herself to seem nervous.

'Deliver it,' Bowling ordered her, curtly.

Yewdall glanced at the package. 'There's no address on it.'

'Here.' Gail Bowling handed Yewdall a slip of paper on which was a typed address.

'I don't know where this is. I'm new in London.'

'You've got a lovely long train journey ahead of you.'

'Oh.'

'Rusher will drive you into Richmond – you needn't change.'

'These are the only clothes I have anyway.'

'Trains, darling ... you need not change trains.'

'Oh ... I see ... sorry.'

'Just stay on the same tube. From Richmond to East Ham, follow the journey on the roof of the carriage, just above the windows.'

'Yes. I've seen them – all the stations all in a line.'

'Get off at East Ham, then walk to the address. Ask a copper if you get lost.' She smirked.

'OK,' Yewdall mumbled and avoided eye contact with the woman.

'Do you have money for the tube?'

'No ... Miss.'

'I like Miss but you can call me Gail – that doesn't mean we're friends. You start getting lippy, you start taking liberties ... well ... let's just say I can be a bad bitch when I need to be and I don't ever get my hands dirty. If someone needs a slap I get Mongoose or Rusher to do the honours ... follow?'

'Yes ... Miss ... er, Gail, yes, I follow.'

Gail Bowling turned to Curtis Yates and said, 'Give her an Adam.' Curtis Yates obediently stood and took a twenty pound note from his wallet and handed it to Yewdall.

'Thank you,' she said, and thought that she had been presented with a useful insight into the Yates firm. He is not the boss, despite all that is said and claimed – The King of Kilburn, indeed. Some king taking orders like that.

'That'll get you to East Ham and then back to Kilburn.'

'I go home?'

'Straight home, like a good girl.'

'Yes, Gail.'

'Just take it to that address. Ring the doorbell, hand it to whoever opens the door and then turn on your pretty heels and get your tail back to Kilburn.'

The journey from Curtis Yates's home in Virginia Water to the underground station in Richmond was passed in silence. Yewdall kept her eyes straight ahead as the windscreen wipers swept slowly back and forth. 'Rusher' Boyd halted outside the tube station and waited for Yewdall to leave the car.

'East Ham?' Yewdall said. Rusher nodded once without looking at her. Yewdall closed the door and walked into the booking office and asked for a ticket to East Ham.

'Right across town, dearie.' The woman behind the glass screen spoke in a chirpy manner as she printed the ticket and scooped up the twenty pound note Yewdall had tended. 'Don't get many wanting to go that far.'The pink ticket slid across the surface of the counter and was followed rapidly by the change she was due. 'Not that far, no we don't.'

Yewdall scooped up the change and did not reply.

The man left the small terraced house on Rutland Street and glanced up at the evening sky, and thought how fortunate that the weather had remained dry, as had been forecast. He let his overcoat hang open and walked to the corner of Waterloo Road, where he turned right and bought a pint carton of milk from the twenty-four hour Asian shop, before returning to Rutland Street. He did not walk up the street, but went past it and took the next parallel road, turned right at the top and turned right again into Rutland Street, thus having walked round the block. Satisfied he was not being followed, and seeing no sign of the yellow BMW, he crossed to where the car had been parked, and in the light of the softly glowing street lamps he carefully picked up six cigarette butts and dropped them into the plastic carrier bag he had been given to carry the carton of milk. He crossed the road again and entered the house. He took the milk from the plastic bag and placed it in the fridge, and then carefully folded the bag containing the six cigarette butts and placed them in a large padded envelope to await their collection. He telephoned the number in London to report the acquisition of the cigarette butts, and then settled down to watch the ten o'clock news before retiring for the night.

Job done.

Penny Yewdall left the underground train at East Ham and walked to the booking hall and to the ticket counter therein. Able to see only the blue shirt and tie of the ticket vendor she asked him the directions to Chaucer Road, East Ham.

'Chaucer,' the man spoke with a warm East London accent, 'that's among the poets, sweetheart ... all the poets, Shelley, Byron. Turn right as you leave the station, up the old High Street ... Chaucer is between Wordsworth and Tennyson.'

Penny Yewdall, having thanked the torso, left the underground station and turned

257

right as directed and into a cold, windy, rainy night. She crossed Plashet Grove and carried on up High Street North, and turned left beyond a low-rise block of inter-war flats and into Chaucer Road, which revealed itself to be a tree-lined late-Victorian terraced development. She went to number twenty-two, conveniently close to High Street North. She walked from the pavement the few feet to the front door, and seeing only a black metal knocker rather than a doorbell, she took hold of it and rapped twice. The door was opened quickly and aggressively by a large West Indian male of, she guessed, about thirty-five years. He eyed her with hostility.

'I have to deliver this package,' she said, holding her ground.

'From? Who from, girl?' The man's attitude was hostile, aggressive, forceful.

'Gail ... a woman called Gail Bowling.'

The man's face softened into a brief smile. 'Where did she give it to you?'

'At her home in Virginia Water.'

'Anyone else there?'

'A man called Curtis, Curtis Yates.'

'OK. Who drove you from her house to the tube station?'

'A geezer called Rusher – don't know any other name for him.'

'Rusher.' The man smiled broadly. 'Alright, girl, you can give me the parcel.' He extended a meaty paw, took it from her and shut the door without a further word.

'You're welcome,' Yewdall said to the closed door. She turned and retraced her steps to the East Ham underground station and bought a ticket to Kilburn. The errand she had run was clearly a test, but the address was one that could be fed to her handler when it was safe for her to do so – she had to assume she was being watched. She passed a vacant telephone kiosk – it would, she thought, be utter folly, crass stupidity, to enter it and phone her handler. What gofer does that? As she walked she began to glimpse the appeal of undercover work. Penny Yewdall had never seen herself as being an adrenalin junkie, but, but ... life seemed suddenly so much more real, more immediate somehow – the I-know-something-that-you-do-not mentality provided her with an unexpected sense of power and a sense of control, so different from the strange detached attitude of mind she had found herself developing when she had been sitting on the steps at Piccadilly underground station begging for spare change. Throughout the rocking, rattling journey home, she had the strange and unsettling sense of being watched. She was definitely a gofer on a trial run, so no phone calls, no postcards sent to the photographic studio in Finchley. But the address, 22 Chaucer Road, East Ham, she committed to memory; that, and the fact that it was Gail Bowling who seemed to wear the trousers in the firm, not Curtis Yates.

'You got my prints by false pretences.' Gail Bowling glared at Vicary. Her indignation was manifest.

'No ... no I didn't, I just asked you to look at an E-FIT.'

'So as to get my fingerprints.'

Harry Vicary shrugged. 'We can't use them to prosecute you.'

'Good, because I am going straight. I did a few stupid things when I was younger but those days are over. I've turned the corner ... put all that behind me.'

'So, working for Curtis Yates is putting all that behind you is it?'

'Yes, it is.' She sniffed. 'I work for a removal company.'

'A removal company which is owned by one of the biggest and slipperiest crooks in the metropolitan area ... and you are working for him, so perhaps you can see our interest?'

'Frankly, I can't.'

'Well, whether or not you can, we've only brought you in for a little chat ... just you ... off the record; in case you want to talk to us.'

'About what? The weather ... damn miserable this rain but it's still mild for the time of year don't you think?'

'About turning Queen's evidence against Curtis Yates.'

'What!' Gail Bowling gasped. 'And you really think that I am in a position to do that?'

'Yes.'

'And you think I would do that.'

'We talked to Clive Sherwin yesterday.'

Gail Bowling scowled but remained silent.

'We made him the same offer.'

'What did he say?'

'So you do know him?'

'I might.'

'Well, to say he was uncooperative would be putting it mildly. He told us what we could do with our offer.'

Gail Bowling smiled.

'But the offer was made and it stands, and we make the same offer to you – turn Queen's evidence ... and we'll be making it to others in your little outfit ... Put Curtis Yates away, go into witness protection, start a new life in a new town somewhere north of the River Trent.'

'North of the Trent!' Gail Bowling sat back in her chair, seemingly amazed at the suggestion. 'I am ... I have never lived anywhere but London. For me the world stops at High Barnet.'

'Well ... elsewhere – Cornwall, Devon, if you like the beautiful south so much.'

'You know what London is like, a collection of little villages – if I moved from Whitechapel to Notting Hill, I'd be just as far from my mates as if I did go north of the Trent.'

'Not as safe though.'

'Anyway ... thanks for the offer. But not interested.'

'Well, think about it, a lot of people want to bring Curtis Yates down ... ourselves ... the Drug Squad ... Internal Revenue and if he falls—'

'If!'

'When he falls, a lot of folk will fall with him. The first two or three to squeal will be doing themselves a huge favour – something for you to think about.'

Gail Bowling stood. 'Just see me to the door.'

Penny Yewdall slept late, then rose nervously, living the part as she had been advised. She left the room wrapped in her coat over her underwear, and padded barefoot along the hallway and into the kitchen. She found Josie Pinder sitting at the table in a short yellow towelling robe, smoking a thin roll-up cigarette and sipping a mug of milkless tea. Her right eye was black and was bruising to the orbit.

'Nice shiner you got there, darlin'.' Yewdall sat in a vacant chair at the table. 'Mind if I join you?'

'Suit yourself.'

'Who punched you?'

'No one punched me. It was a slap, and I don't mean a push, I mean a slap – flat hand, side of my head, blood flows into the old eye socket; makes it look like a punch but it was a slap.'

'That true?' Yewdall sounded surprised, though she had seen the like many times before, usually upon women slapped by an angered partner, but once upon a man, and which had been inflicted by a powerfully built woman whom he had taken as his wife. 'So who hit you?'

Josie Pinder drew on the cigarette and inclined her head upwards, indicating the rooms on the first floor. Specifically, Yewdall realized, the room she shared with Sonya

Clements.

'So why stay with her?'

Josie Pinder shrugged. 'Why does anyone stay with someone who knocks them about? It was my fault ... a sense of loyalty – misplaced, I know – lack of self-respect ... it wears you down so you get to accept it as a way of life.'

'You seem bright, like smart in the head, worth more than this.'

'Oh, I am smart, Manchester University would you believe? But I was too working class and I was too close to home. I came from Salford, next door to Manchester. One bus from the Uni to the city centre, but only if it was raining, other times I'd walk it in twenty minutes. One bus to Salford, then I could walk home. If I had gone further away, like to Swansea or Canterbury, then I might have battled against the snobbery working-class students meet at university ... but I met her at a dykes' club in Manchester – thought I'd met my soul mate, so I jacked in civil engineering and came south with 'er.'

'Civil engineering?'

'Yes, that was another thing, as well as the snobbery, as well as being little working-class Nellie from the Dellie among these privately educated types, I was penetrating a male bastion. It's getting better but engineering is still a male preserve ... largely ... no matter what university. So this is the south – hardly what it's cracked up to be. A room in a house like this and a black eye for touching her. She can touch me all she likes but I can't touch her. I'm the female ... she does ... I am done to, I need to remember my place.'

'I know what you mean. Still think that you should leave.'

'Where?' She dragged deeply on the cigarette. 'Like where?'

'Shelters ... ? Back to Salford?'

'Can't go home – not like this ... half-starved, dressed in rags – such an admission of failure. If I go to a shelter I'll get dragged back here.'

'Who by?'

'Yates. Who do you think?' She lowered her voice and glanced around her. 'These walls have ears ... seems like it anyway.'

'You're paranoid.'

'Believe me, there must be hidden microphones ... Mary, is it?'

'Penny.'

'I'm Josie. That accent, Stoke-on-Trent?'

'Yes, that way ... the Potteries.'

'Been in London long?'

'Just less than two years. Can't go back for

the same reason as you ... too proud to admit defeat.'

'It traps you like that, London does. That's what Gaynor's problem was.'

'Gaynor?'

'The Welsh girl, she had the room you're in. She was murdered in there ... remember ... we told you...'

'Yes...'

'Best not to ask too many questions, but like we said, she was brought home by the guy whose room it really was – brought her in off the street, just to keep her safe. He was going to send her home and he also wanted away from Yates. They both made the wrong sort of noises ... so follow my drift?'

'Yes, I think so. Am I in danger?'

'We all are – that's why her majesty upstairs is on edge. She runs this house for Yates; she tells him everything that goes on here.' Josie Pinder's voice dropped to a whisper. 'She would have told him about Mickey Dalkeith and Gaynor planning to leave.'

'Why didn't he want them to leave?' Yewdall paused. 'Sorry, questions ... I shouldn't ask ... you're right ... that's good advice.'

'Best remember it, but Mickey was a long-time member of Yates's firm, more than a gofer ... not real high up but high up enough to know where all the bodies is buried, makes him a liability. Yates had Gaynor strangled in Mickey Dalkeith's room so Mickey would get fingered for it if he ran, but Mickey does not come home as expected ... turns out he went to sleep on Hampstead Heath instead. He told Sonya where he was going, and Yates and one of his heavies went after him ... followed a set of footprints on the off chance and came across Mickey Dalkeith lying there. So I was told, anyway.'

'Asleep?'

'In the snow ... hypothermia ... suicide, I reckon. He must have thought it was his only exit.'

'I see.'

'So the police came here investigating Mickey's death and found Gaynor's body, put two and two together – Mickey's slain Gaynor and then topped himself by lying down in the snow rather than do life. So Yates is well pleased. He's off the hook and Mickey's not a threat to him no more. But things have not gone away for some reason I don't know about. The filth is still sniffing around Yates and Bowling.'

'Bowling?'

'His female oppo. Watch her if you run

into her; they say she's worse than him.'

'OK, thanks for the warning.'

'So that's why she's on edge.' Josie Pinder pointed to the room she shared with Sonya Clements. 'She came back from the garage yesterday. She had to watch one of Yates's heavies get a kicking.'

'The garage?'

'Yes, a lock-up really, under the railway arches, down the East End somewhere. I've never been there myself. He'd been lifted by the filth who took him in for a chat. He says he didn't say anything to the filth but he got a kicking anyway as a warning. He was one of the heavies who iced Dunwoodie, so he can damage Yates if he wants to do so. You know, turn Queen's evidence, go into witness protection. This guy, Clive someone, he swore blind he didn't tell the filth anything, but he got a kicking anyway ... like just a gentle – a very, very gentle – reminder not to ever say anything ... not ever.'

'Blimey.'

'So she came back shaking like a leaf 'cos she'd seen a kicking before, but not like that, she says. Went on all day, it did. They stopped for lunch and carried on in the afternoon. They left him on the pavement a mile or so away. Let him be found and taken to hospital. He'll still be bruised in six months' time and every waking movement for him will be agony. But you'll see a kicking.'

'I will?'

'Yes. You're a gofer aren't you?'

'Am I?'

'Have you done an errand, delivered a message or a parcel?'

'A parcel.'

'OK, so you're a gofer, you're in the firm. You'll be collected to witness a kicking if someone gets out of order, and they tell you that's what'll happen to you if you get left field. Being a girl makes no difference.'

There was the sound of movement from upstairs.

'She's getting up.' Josie Pinder grimaced. 'She'll want her tea.' She stood and partly filled the battered aluminium kettle with water, then ignited a gas ring on the oven and placed the kettle on the flames.

'How do I get out?' Yewdall asked plaintively. 'This is getting too much for me.'

'You don't, sweetheart. Feet first possibly. Other than that you don't get out.' Josie Pinder reached for a clean mug and placed a little milk into it. 'You're in ... and believe me ... you'd better keep your pretty little nose clean, as clean as a whistle. Cleaner.'

Vicary sat down in the chair in front of the

desk in the interview suite at New Scotland Yard. 'We meet again, Mr Yates.'

'Seems so.' Curtis Yates was dressed casually in closely fitting casual clothes that showed off his muscular build. 'So what's this about?'

'A chat.' Vicary smiled. 'Just a chat.'

'Then why has my client been arrested?' The middle-aged man wearing a pinstripe suit who sat next to Yates spoke with a soft voice, which Vicary thought could be disarming if he let it. It seemed to Vicary that he was the embodiment of Teddy Roosevelt's advice to 'speak softly and carry a big stick', a man, thought Vicary, not be underestimated.

'Because I am doing him a favour.' Vicary smiled at the lawyer, one Kieran Worth, of Worth, Lockwood and Company. The Rolex on his left wrist spoke clearly of the level of fees he commanded. 'If he'll let me.'

'You want to do me a favour?' Yates sneered. 'Don't go putting yourself out for nothing.'

'Well, you scratch my back,' Vicary replied calmly. 'But we've been investigating you.'

'I know you have. Don't got nowhere, do you?'

'Closer than you think. You know we can link you to the murder of Rosemary Hal-

270

kier. Remember her? Ten years ago now she was your girl. We can link you to Michael Dalkeith's death, and you're there in the background of Gaynor Davies' murder. You see our interest, Curtis? You don't mind if I call you Curtis?'

'Don't mind.'

'We really want to talk to Rusher. Can't remember his name but it's in the file. It's quite thick now ... the file ... our witness gave a good description of him. Quite close when Rusher was battering Mr Dunwoodie to death in the alley. The geezer with Rusher said, "That's enough, Rusher", but Rusher kept on battering away saying, "The boss wants him dead". So, if we can find Rusher ... and he tells us you're the boss in question ... well, then, then you go down, for a long stretch. All this smoke that surrounds you, Curtis, this odour of suspicion, it smells like Billingsgate Market at the end of a long summer's day. Have you ever smelled rotten fish, Curtis? Got a distinct smell all its own it has, like fear. You must have smelled fear from someone ... quite often I imagine.'

'Maybe...'

Vicary leaned forward. 'You see, Curtis, it's time to think ... now ... off the record – off the record, you won't be prosecuted for all the men and women you've chilled or had chilled. So in a sense you'll get away with those murders.'

Yates smiled.

Vicary held up a finger. 'Don't get cocky, Curtis, because we don't have to prosecute you for all of them.' He paused. 'Just think about that. You've only got one life, so all we need is one conviction, and right now we're looking at three murders which are covered in your dabs.'

'You can't link me to them.'

'Yet.' Vicary smiled briefly. 'Not yet. Just needs one of your firm to do a deal for themselves. Like I said, just one conviction will get you a life stretch. I tell you, if I was one of your firm, and I thought you were going to topple, then I'd be squealing very loudly, very, very loudly. You can forget getting out in five years; career crims like you don't get past the parole board.'

'That's coercion.' Worth smelled of expensive aftershave.

'It's the truth.' Vicary turned to Worth. 'I am just doing Mr Curtis the favour I said I would do for him if he let me. Now, should he wish to turn Queen's evidence...'

'Use your loaf,' Yates sneered.

'It depends how much you want to rescue,' Vicary explained. 'You see, it's not just the loss of liberty ... you'll be in high security, no soft category D for you ... Parkhurst, Durham, Peterhead ... right up there in Scotland, and in the far north of same. Porridge for breakfast and veggies which have had all the goodness boiled out of them for lunch, with a bit of meat. Same for supper. No women – I know how you like the ladies – and nothing to come out to.'

'What do you mean?'

'A proceeds of crime order. Get a team of forensic accountants into your books, your computer database, and everything you cannot prove you came by legitimately can be seized: house, contents therein, cars, everything. The lot, the whole works. That's how it works. You do twenty as a guest of Her Majesty, come out, fit as a fiddle after all those years of prison life and do you go back to your posh house in Virginia Water? No ... no, you don't. You come out to a hostel for the homeless and destitute – Salvation Army living. They're not in the *Michelin Guide*, but it's a roof, and they serve meals on time ... just like in prison, But by then you'll be used to that, because you'll be well and truly institutionalized.'

Curtis Yates's pallor paled.

'Of course you could avoid that. Jump before you're pushed.'

'I'll still end up in the slammer.'

'Yes ... yes, you will, but the difference is that if you jump, you jump into a safety net. A guilty plea will work towards a parole, but if you're pushed, that can be messy ... you fall from a great height on to a hard surface.'

Yates remained silent.

'So far we've chatted to Clive Sherwin and Gail Bowling. You've got good friends there, they didn't tell us anything, but that's only the first two, and you've got a lot of geezers working for you. We still want to talk to Rusher, but really it just needs one to see sense and you're on your way to the Old Bailey.' Vicary paused. 'Go to the pub to-night.'

'The pub?'

'Yes, up the East End, with the villains, or wherever you sup in Virginia Water. Buy a beer and then look around you, and then think that you can't take this for granted because it's liberty. Think that it could be the last time you see the inside of an English pub again, and choose what you want to watch on the TV for the last time ... and retire for the night when you want to ... also for the last – well, maybe the last – time for twenty years, because tomorrow at seven a.m. I'll be knocking on your door with a warrant for your arrest.'

'Tomorrow!'

'Or the next day, or the day after that, but stop taking the good life for granted. We're closing in on you, Curtis. You should think about working for yourself.'

SEVEN

The man let the phone ring twice before he picked it up.

'Forensic laboratory, sir.' The voice on the other end of the phone line was crisp, efficient.

'Yes?'

'Just to let you know beforehand that the DNA tests on the cigarette butts you sent came back negative. No record at all.'

'I see.'

'Just thought I'd let you know in advance. We'll be faxing the report in an hour or two, once it's been written up.'

'OK,' the man replied warmly, 'appreciate the notice.'

He replaced the phone and returned his attention to his monthly statistical returns.

Penny Yewdall slept late. She woke and looked about her in the shadows and the gloom of the room in which the Welsh girl had been murdered – the room which was now her room. She felt isolated. Alone. Vulnerable. She said as loudly as she dared, 'I am a copper. I am a copper. I am a damn good copper, police woman Yewdall of the Murder and Serious Crime Squad, New Scotland Yard.' She rose and clawed on a few items of clothing – underwear, jeans, a tee shirt – and walked into the kitchen, where she found a nervous looking Billy Kemp, whom she'd met in passing, sitting at the table, occupying the same chair that Josie Pinder had occupied the previous morning, and, like Josie Pinder, he also drank a mug of tea and smoked a hand-rolled cigarette.

'We have to stay in today, you and me.' He spoke with a trembling voice.

'Have to?'

'Yes. The manager of WLM Rents called round earlier and told me that we have to stay in. You and me.'

'Why?' Penny Yewdall sank into a vacant chair at the table.

'Dunno, but I think someone's going to get a kicking.'

'Oh...'

'And we're going to watch.'

'We...?' Yewdall's voice failed her.

'We. I'm in the same boat as you. I'm a gofer being trained up. Trained and tested.

I've delivered a few packages, three in all.'

'I delivered one – to an address in East Ham.'

'Chaucer Road?'

'Yes.'

'Same as me. I don't reckon it's some big important address, they're just testing us. They won't let us go to really important addresses until we're further in.'

'I thought you were established. It was just an impression I had.'

'Yes, I have been here a while ... just not getting anywhere with Yates. He's still not certain of me. Have you had a slap yet?'

'No.'

'I have, Yates slapped me round the head and punched me on the nose ... just enough to make it bleed and said, "No one leaves me, remember that".' Billy Kemp paused and gulped some tea. 'Then he sent a couple of guys to check on my home address in Norwich.'

'Think they did the same to my old dad in Stoke.'

'Yes, I think that he's not checking on you so much as letting you know he can get to your kin if you do a moonlight.'

Yewdall gasped.

'Well ... maybe he's doing both. Checking on you and also letting you know he can hurt your family if you allow yourself to drop off his radar. I'm in too deep.'

'Me too.'

'What do I do? What do we do? That bitch upstairs, the butch lesbian, Sonya Clements, she told me that you only get to be a proper gofer, get paid and all that, once you've seen someone get a kicking. Then you're in the firm. Bottom rung of the ladder, but you're in. But you need to see what happens to someone who gets out of order.'

'I don't want to watch,' Yewdall pleaded.

'You think I do? But keep your voice down, Clements tells Yates everything. You can't cough in this house without her telling Yates. She'll have been through your room.'

'I thought someone had been in.'

'It will have been her, poking round while you were out begging.'

Yewdall paused, then asked, 'What about the Welsh girl?'

'Gaynor? What about her?'

'Well … Josie told me she was murdered in that front room.'

'Yes, one night. Yates doesn't kill in daylight, it's just his thing.'

'So why do you also have to watch a kicking?'

'Different story, I think. Don't know but I think she was just … used … she hadn't gone

279

left field. Curtis Yates needed a body to frame the guy who had the room before you, Mickey Dalkeith by name ... nice geezer, but if Josie said "we" witnessed it, she must have meant her and Sonya Clements. I wasn't there.'

'I see.'

'So how much money have you got?'

'About six or seven pounds.'

'I've got about ten.'

'So what are you thinking?'

'The pub.' He glanced at the clock on the wall – it read ten minutes to eleven. 'Get dressed. ... walk slowly – they'll just have opened by the time we get there.'

'I thought we had to stay in?'

'They're coming for us at one thirty, and like I said, we can't hide anywhere. I think I'd rather wait in the pub and have a stiff one or two. I'll need it if I am going to watch someone get kicked to death.'

'To death!'

'Well it could go that far, whether they intend it or not. I mean they kicked J.J. Dunwoodie to death.'

'So I heard. He wasn't even in the firm...'

'Of course he was.' Billy Kemp smiled. 'He was well in, just played the wide-eyed innocent.'

'I never knew him.'

'It happened just before you moved here. He was battered to death in an alley close to the office where he worked.'

'This is one hell of a mess.'

'Where to go?' Billy Kemp sighed. 'What to do? Wonder how long it took to batter him to death?'

Yewdall and Billy Kemp sat in the pub. Yewdall thought that they must have made a strange couple – she so much larger than he, and clearly older – sitting together, side by side, yet saying little. It was early in the day and the landlord scowled at them, but they were paying, and the licensed retail trade is struggling. It was, Yewdall noticed, a clean pub, with a deep carpet, a highly polished wooden bar and wall panels containing sepia prints of Kilburn in a different era – an era of horse-drawn trams and drays, men in bowler hats and women in ankle-length skirts and dresses, and of solid, medium-rise buildings, many of which, she had noticed, still remained.

Yewdall's mind worked feverishly ... what to do ... what to do ... to rescue the quaking Billy Kemp and walk with him into the police station? Would that prevent what was going to happen to some wretched soul in 'the garage'? No, she thought, no, it prob-

281

ably wouldn't and what had she got to offer? An address in East Ham which was clearly used only as a practice drop – the police would find nothing there if they raided. The intelligence that kickings took place in a lock-up called 'the garage', that Michael Dalkeith did not murder Gaynor Davies, that he was in fact rescuing her and was going to be fitted up for the murder, that ... that might be worth blowing her cover for if Michael Dalkeith was still alive and under suspicion. In the end, she decided to remain silent and keep her cover. She wanted something to offer for her time. It was early days yet and she still had nothing to connect Yates with anything.

'We'd better be getting back,' Billy Kemp said when the large clock above the bar read one o'clock. 'We'll have to fill our mouths with toothpaste to cover the smell of booze. Mind, we can say it was from last night.'

'I'll be back.' Yewdall rose and walked into the ladies' toilet. Ensuring that all the cubicles were empty she stood in front of a large frosted mirror, mounted within an elaborate plaster surround, and fixed herself in the eye, and said, 'I ... am ... a ... police ... officer...' She then returned to where Billy was, by then, standing; waiting obediently, Labrador-like, she thought.

Yewdall and Kemp returned to the house and sat in the kitchen after putting large quantities of toothpaste into their mouths as they had planned. They waited in silence. At twenty-five past the hour a key was heard turning in the lock of the front door; heavy footfall tramped down the hallway and the kitchen door was pushed open. A tall, well-built, muscular man stood in the doorway. He looked at Yewdall and then at Kemp and said, 'Come on.'

They rose and followed him out of the house. In the road, double-parked, was a black Mercedes with the rear door opened. Without a word being said, Kemp and Yewdall slid into the back seat. The door was closed behind them. Yewdall tried to open her door but couldn't. The child locks had been put on; a useful piece of kit for parents and felons alike. The man who had collected them sat in the front passenger seat, and the driver started the car and pulled away.

Yewdall sat in silence but took careful note of the route. They drove north-west out of London, past the wealthy, well-set suburbs, out to Hemel Hempstead, and then to a village Yewdall noticed was called Water End.

Water End.

Water End.

Water End.

She committed the name to memory.

The phone on Harry Vicary's desk warbled twice. He picked it up leisurely. 'Vicary,' he said.

'We have a problem...' the voice on the other end of the line said.

'Who's we?'

'I'm Penny Yewdall's handler.'

'Yes.'

'We got the DNA results from the cigarette butts – just been delivered.'

'Sorry, you have lost me ... calm down...'

'Sorry, we fixed Penny up with a false ID – a home in Hanley in the Potteries; a retired officer from the Staffordshire force occupied the home address posing as her father.'

'Yes.'

'She was checked out by a couple of heavies who sat outside her "father's" house in a car ... then they emptied the ashtray in the road.'

'Ah ... hence the DNA results,' Vicary observed, 'I see now.'

'Yes, they came back no trace, which was unusual, but not only that, the DNA is from four people not two ... and two of those four are female...'

'Oh no!'

'Yes ... oh yes ... those two geezers must have picked up the cigarette ends from the ground, knowing we'd pick them up for DNA sampling. She's been rumbled. From day one, she was rumbled as being a cop.'

'Now they're playing us ... taunting us. Where is she?'

'Don't know.'

'You don't know!'

'Either down Piccadilly panhandling, or at the house in Kilburn. I'll go to Piccadilly.'

'OK, I'll take a team to the house. I hope we're in time.'

'Praying might be better than hoping,' the handler said, but by this time Vicary had slammed the handset down and was reaching for his hat and coat, and calling for assistance.

The driver threaded the Mercedes-Benz through the village of Water End and continued for a mile, Yewdall guessed, and then turned right, directly opposite a thatch-roofed, white-painted cottage with the date 1610 AD above the door, which caused Yewdall to smile inwardly – a four-hundred-year-old cottage, what better landmark? The metalled surface of the road eventually gave out to an unsurfaced road, liberally covered with gravel to provide some grip for car tyres, Yewdall assumed, and possibly to give warning of approaching vehicles. The track led shortly to a collection of farm buildings – a house, a barn, outbuildings – which formed an L-shape around the courtyard. Parked on the courtyard was a collection of vehicles. Yewdall noted a Rolls-Royce, mud bespattered, a Ford Granada, a Land Rover and a transit van. The driver halted the Mercedes beside the van and the occupant of the passenger seat got out and opened the rear door. He knelt down, and quickly and efficiently pulled Yewdall's shoes from her feet. Then he addressed Billy Kemp, saying brusquely, 'Your shoes too, matey.' Kemp obediently leaned forward and began to tug at his laces. Once the hard-faced man was in possession of both pairs of shoes he said, 'You'll get these back when you need them. Right, out...'

Yewdall and Billy Kemp slid one by one out of the car and stepped gingerly on to the cold, rough surface of the courtyard. The man then tossed their shoes into the rear of the Mercedes and shut the door. 'OK,' he said, 'this way.' He led them across the courtyard, walking comfortably in heavy working shoes, accompanied by the man who had driven the Mercedes. Yewdall and

Kemp followed, walking with difficulty. Yewdall had not realized until then how disabling it can be to be relieved of one's footwear.

Upon reaching the barn, the driver of the car opened a small wooden door set in the larger barn door and entered. The second man stood to one side and indicated for Yewdall and Kemp to go through the entrance. Then he followed them and shut the door behind him. The interior of the barn was illuminated by a single bulb set on the wall by the door, which left the greater part of the interior of the barn in darkness, but what it did illuminate was a man and a woman standing together, a youth on the floor dressed only in his underpants and whimpering with fear, a domestic bath filled with water, and various items of machinery.

'Nice one, Rusher.' The man smiled at the driver's companion who had occupied the passenger seat during the journey from Kilburn to the farm. 'Any trouble?'

'No, boss, they was as good as gold, they was.'

'Let's hope they stay like that.' The man addressed Yewdall, 'You know who I am?'

'No...' Yewdall whispered. 'Not your name, sir ... but I was in your house...'

The man smiled. 'Course you do, you're

just being cagey. You know, don't you lad?'

'Mr Yates.'

'And the lady...'

'Miss Bowling.'

'Yes ... course, we've all met before, ain't we?'

'Y–yes...'

'Yes, course we have. We want you to watch this ... this ... this little toerag–'Yates pointed to the whimpering youth – 'this thing. He couldn't pull a bird he couldn't, so what does he do? He half-inches off me to buy himself a brass for the night. Went down King's Cross with bundles of smackers – nothing wrong with that you might say – but the problem is those smackers were not his, were they?'

'I was going to put it back,' the youth wailed.

'Course you were ... course you were ... but that's not the point. Now I don't mind a thief, not until he half-inches from me ... then that is like well out of order ... it is really well out of order, and the bottle it must have taken to believe he could get away with it.' Yates took a running kick at the youth who doubled up under the impact to his stomach. 'That is just so out of order ... so out of order ... it ain't exactly what you'd call polite ... not polite at all ... not respectful like, not to a man who took him off the street and gave him a drum and a job. Alright, Rusher, make this one quick ... you too Henry.'

Rusher and Henry – who had driven Yewdall and Kemp to the farm – advanced on the helpless youth and proceeded to kick him about the head and body, but particularly about the head. The youth very quickly became lifeless but continued to emit gurgling sounds, which after a period of less then five minutes, Yewdall estimated, ceased.

'That it?' Yates asked when Rusher and Henry stopped kicking.

'Yeah...' Rusher showed no sign of being out of breath. He and Henry both gave the impression that they could have carried on kicking the youth for a further half hour before showing any sign of fatigue. 'It's done.'

'OK.' Yates looked down at the bloody, pulped face of the youth. During the assault, neither he nor Bowling had made any movement or made any facial expression that Yewdall had noticed, but rather, both had stood as calmly as if waiting for a bus. Detachment, she thought, was just not the word. 'Give him a bath.'

Rusher and Henry lifted up the body of

the youth and placed it face down in the bath – immersing him so that just his calves and feet showed.

'That'll sort him if the kicking didn't,' Gail Bowling commented.

'Oh, the kicking did it alright.' Yates smiled. 'They're good boys but you can never be too sure...'

'Is he going to the building site?' Bowling asked. 'The old concrete coffin?'

'No ... he's staying here ... I'm going to have him planted out the back. I've got the hole dug.' Yates advanced on Yewdall and, taking a length of chain from his coat pocket, he wrapped it tightly round one of her wrists and secured it with a small brass padlock, and then speedily and efficiently wound the other end of the chain equally tightly round her other wrist, and similarly secured it with a brass padlock, thus holding her wrists together, six inches apart. 'I want to show you something, blossom,' he said smiling. 'Come with me.' He put his arm in hers and led her gently out of the barn. Walking with discomfort Yewdall was led from the barn to the meadow behind the barn wherein stood a line of short trees. Close to where Yates and Yewdall stood were three large holes about five feet long, three feet wide and three feet deep.

Beside each hole was a sapling wrapped in newspaper.

'Flowering cherry,' Yates announced with pride, 'my favourite tree ... the blossom in spring time ... exquisite. They don't bear fruit, so it will never be a cherry orchard, but it is a lovely old tree.'

'So why bring me up here?'

'Rare old treat, darlin'.' Yates smiled. 'You're sort of a special customer...'

'Cust...' Yewdall stammered.

'Yeah ... for want of a better way of putting it, here you go, girl, choose your hole.'

Yewdall pulled away from Yates but he held her close. 'What's the rush, darlin'? One for the youth we just chilled, one for Billy Kemp ... he's getting to know what's in store for him right now...' Just at that moment a high-pitched cry was heard from the barn. 'Ah, reckon he's just been told. No one will hear. We let dogs out at night, keeps the poachers off the land. You can scream your lungs out tonight. So, what do you think ... the middle one?'

'Why?'

'Why you? What have you done? Is that what you're asking?'

'Yes...'

'It's because you're the filth, ain't you?'

Yewdall went cold, and a chill shot down

291

her spine; she felt a hollowness in her stomach.

'You came from nowhere, and you came right in the middle of the filth asking questions. Just a little grubby but not grubby enough ... it takes weeks ... not a day or two ... and you're taller, fitter, more healthy looking than most street dwellers ... and you were careful not to ask questions.'

Yewdall looked around her, the winter landscape, the trees, the low sky, the cawing rooks all seemed so much more real, so much more immediate somehow.

'And your old man in Stoke,' Yates continued. 'We paid him a visit ... cor blimey ... he had everything but "Police" stamped on his forehead. Full of confidence when two strange geezers knocked on his door ... no fear ... no concern for his safety, just full of anger towards you like he was reading from a script.'

Yates took a packet of cigarettes from his pocket and took two, lit them with a gold lighter, and pushed one between Yewdall's lips. Yewdall surprised herself by accepting it, and inhaled the smoke.

'It's paranoia, darling,' Yates explained as he turned Yewdall around and began walking her back to the barn, 'paranoia ... that keeps us alive. Suspect everyone ... trust no one ... you need to believe that everyone is out to get you because they are ... cops, blaggers ... dog eat dog.'

Yewdall's head sank, her feet were numb with cold.

'Well, I got to say thanks for not claiming you're not a cop – that would be really naughty of you, darling. I have more than two brain cells despite all that vodka I have thrown down my neck. Been doing that like there's no tomorrow, but that's my look out. I'll be outliving you. How old are you darlin'?'

'Twenty-five.' Yewdall looked around her at the winter landscape.

'Twenty-five,' Yates repeated. 'I could do with being that young, but with this loaf–' he tapped the side of his head – 'cor ... I mean, cor blimey, just think of that ... all this know-how and a twenty-five-year-old body, I'd be the King of London, never mind Kilburn. Well, it comes to us all sooner or later, for you it'll be sooner. It was Sonya who put us on to you ... you were just too clean and well-preserved.'

'Sonya?'

'Yeah, the big girl at the house. She's a good girl ... put us on to Billy too, she did. She's doing alright for herself she is, she's set to climb.'

'What about Billy? He's just a boy.'

'He's just a boy with a loud mouth ... too much rabbit; he just can't keep his old north and south shut. He's a liability we can do without.'

'I feel sick...' Yewdall stumbled on the rough surface of the meadow.

'It's the smoke, it's not good for you,' Yates laughed, then he paused and said, 'All ... all because of that idiot Dalkeith. I told him to bury a body here, in this meadow, but what does he do? Buries her on Hampstead Heath. Yes, he digs a hole here and plants a tree, knowing I would not dig it up and check. Rosie Halkier, she should have been down there at the bottom end.' He turned to look at the meadow. 'Down there with that meddling cook, Tessie O'Shea. They were plotting against me and Gail, but we got to them first, and if Dalkeith had done the job like I told him, none of this would have come out. He left me with a right old mess to clean up, and you ... you'll never see twenty-six ... you've got Irish Mickey Dalkeith to thank for that. Well, let's get back to the barn, it's cold out here.'

Upon re-entering the barn, Yewdall saw that Billy Kemp lay curled up on the floor clutching his stomach, breathing with difficulty.

'He tried to do a runner,' Gail Bowling explained, 'so Rusher tapped him.'

'Nice one, Rusher.' Yates smiled approvingly. 'Better fasten him, Henry.'

'Yes, boss.' Henry took a length of chain and padlocked one end to a large item of machinery, and the other end he padlocked round Billy Kemp's ankle.

Yates pushed Penny Yewdall over towards Billy Kemp and, taking a small key, unlocked the chain round her left wrist, and then padlocked the end to the chain which held Billy Kemp captive.

'That's a nice sight.' Gail Bowling gazed approvingly on the captive forms of Penny Yewdall and Billy Kemp. 'That really is a very nice sight.'

'When do we do them?' Yates turned to Bowling.

'Tomorrow. Tomorrow afternoon late, early evening, when dusk is falling ... give them time to think about things. Bet you never thought your last twenty-four hours in this life would be spent in a barn in Hertfordshire, did you, Constable?' Bowling asked with a smile. 'And such a pretty girl ... what a waste.'

Yewdall did not reply.

'Thank you for not telling us that we won't get away with it ... because we will. We have been getting away with it for years ... but you've seen the cherry trees ... no one knows what they mean. No one knows what's underneath them. If you scream ... well, you can scream, because no one will hear you, but if you do, Henry will come and tap you, won't you, Henry?'

'Damn right, I will.'

'Packer will be in the house keeping warm but awake all night, won't you, Henry? Just one mighty blow from his fist to your stomach will keep you quiet. I mean, look at him–' Gail Bowling pointed to the curled-up figure of Billy Kemp – 'he won't be saying anything for a while ... and shouting ... well, forget it.

'So, we'll leave you – we have a dinner party to attend; got to get back home and get dressed for it ... but there's nothing like a trip to the country to put an edge on your appetite.'

Bowling and Yates left the barn. Henry Packer followed shortly afterwards, turning off the light and shutting the door behind him.

Yewdall tugged at the chain and then gave up. The only sound was the wheezing Billy Kemp.

Harry Vicary forced the door of 123 Claremont Road and stormed into the hall, followed by Brunnie and Ainsclough, and four uniformed constables. He yelled, 'Police!' and then turned to the constables. 'Search the house. Bring everyone down to the kitchen.'

The only person in the house at the time proved to be Sonya Clements, who was dragged protesting into the kitchen.

'So where is she?'

'Who?'

'My officer!'

'Your officer?'

'Yes...' Vicary snarled, 'my officer, Penny Yewdall.'

'Penny's a cop!' Clements gasped.

'Yes ... Penny's a cop and Yates has her. Yates is finished and everyone associated with him is finished too. So where is she?'

'Don't know! Honest. She was driven off about an hour ago.'

'Who drove her off!'

'Dunno ... Rusher did ... her and Billy Kemp.'

'Where did they go?'

'I don't know ... look, I'm just a girl, I don't know anything.'

'But you know Rusher works for Yates!'

'Yes...'

'So what do you do for Yates?'

'Just a gofer, fetch and deliver stuff – just little stuff. Do what I'm told.'

'Take her in, suspicion of handling stolen property.' Vicary paused. 'That'll do for now ... but listen you,' he addressed Sonya, 'listen, we are wrapping up Yates. He's going down and he'll be well tucked-up for a long time. So right now it's just handling stolen goods, but if anything happens to Penny it could be conspiracy to murder a police officer ... and when a firm like Yates's firm starts collapsing, everyone is out to save themselves. Everyone starts squealing like a sty full of stuck pork, it's a hell of a racket, and we'll then find out what has gone on and who has done what. So, do some thinking while you're in the van and start working for yourself. Alright, take her away!' Two constables dragged a wide-eyed and worried looking Sonya Clements out of the house and into a police van.

'Take the house apart.' Vicary spoke to Ainsclough and the two remaining officers. 'I don't know what you are looking for but take the place apart.' He tapped Frankie Brunnie on the shoulder and said, 'Come with me.'

Vicary walked aggressively out of the house, turned on to Fernhead Road, and headed to the offices of WLM Rents. He and Brunnie entered aggressively. The manager stood reverentially as they entered, and managed to say, 'Good afternoon, gent—' before Vicary grabbed his lapels, pulled him over the desk and threw him on the floor. 'Penny Yewdall,' he shouted. 'Where is she?'

'Who?' The youthful manager looked shocked and frightened. He was one Nicholas Batty, by his name badge.

'My officer!'

'Your officer,' he stammered.

'Yes, Metropolitan Police ... and my officer was driven away about an hour ago by Curtis Yates's thugs...'

'I just look after the office.'

'Sure?'

'Yes...'

'We'll find out, we'll find out everything.' Brunnie leaned forward, and taking the man by his lapels, once again, he pulled him to his feet and brushed the man's jacket. 'You're out of work, sunshine.'

'Out...'

'Of work,' Vicary completed the sentence for him. 'Yates is finished, his firm is on the way out and we'll find out the extent of everyone's involvement.'

'Including yours, Nicky boy,' Brunnie added, 'including yours.'

Vicary's mobile vibrated. He took it out of

his pocket and snatched it open. 'Yes!' He listened. He then said, 'It doesn't look like she's here either.' He snapped the phone shut. He turned to Brunnie. 'She's not at Piccadilly.'

'So now what?' Brunnie kept hold of Nicholas Batty's arm.

'Don't know ... bring him with us.'

'On what charge, boss?'

'Dunno ... we'll think of one – can't leave him out here now he knows Penny's a copper. You got the keys to this office?'

'Desk drawer.'

Vicary strode across the floor to the desk, opened the drawer and took out a bunch of keys. 'These?'

'Yes.'

'Right.' He walked back to where Brunnie and Batty stood and handed the keys to Brunnie. 'Check in the back room, then lock up and give the keys back to me ... and you, start to think about working for yourself, Nicholas. Curtis Yates is finished; he's got nothing to hold over you now.'

The long afternoon stretched into an even longer night. Billy Kemp, to whom Penny Yewdall was chained, had eventually, but only eventually, stopped asking questions which Yewdall could not answer – 'Which

300

one of us will they kill first?', 'Will they drown us like they drowned him?', 'Will our bodies ever be found?', 'Will anyone know what happened?' He then gave up the futile tugging of the chain, seemed to curl up into a ball and settled into a prolonged whimpering, which he kept up until the dawn.

In time, a certain calm, a certain peace settled over Penny Yewdall. So, she thought, so it has come to this – an early death at the hands of thieves and gangsters, but it was also a death she felt proud to die ... for the police force. She had joined to serve, and had joined accepting the risks therein. Not perhaps as much of a risk as is faced by those who enlist in the armed services, but nonetheless police officers not infrequently lose their lives when on duty. Penny Yewdall, noticing that sounds appeared louder, smells stronger as she waited to die, realized that she was not worried for herself – she had hoped for a quick and painless death when her time came, and like the whimpering youth she did not relish the thought of drowning, the panic ... the struggle ... the bursting lungs ... and likewise she did not want to die by falling from a great height, nor by incineration – but her worry turned to fear for her parents, her real, actual parents, still alive and living in retirement on the coast, and her sister and brother. Her family must know what had happened to her; they would need a grave to visit, a place to lay wreaths and a place where they could gather and grieve, but they were not going to have that. She would disappear, leaving them not knowing what had happened to her. They would never know peace. They would be in permanent distress. It was for them that she worried, endlessly fretting while her earthly remains putrefied under a sapling of a flowering cherry tree, so pretty in the spring, in a meadow in Hertfordshire. That was the worry – she felt for her family; aggravated by the sense of guilt that she had, somehow, betrayed them.

It became cold that night. Very cold. In the barn rats rustled about. Outside in the still air, an owl hooted.

Victor Swannell stepped nimbly out of the drizzle and off the greasy pavement, entered the main entrance of the London Hospital and was immediately assailed by the strong smell of formaldehyde. He consulted the hospital directory and took the stairs, in preference to the lift, to the second floor. Upon reaching the second floor he turned left and entered the ward, and approached the nursing station. He showed his ID. 'I was told a patient wishes to see the police as a matter of urgency. A man called Sherwin ... Clive Sherwin.'

'Ah, yes.' The senior of the two nurses at the station stood. She was one Sister Jewell, by her name badge, which was fixed perfectly horizontal on the lapel of her uniform. She was a short, finely built woman – serious-minded, thought Swannell – the sort of nursing sister who is always right all the time about everything and a terror of trainees. 'I'll take you to him. We have put him in a private room, wholly for the benefit of the other patients I might add. He would distress them.'

'Distress them?'

'You'll see what I mean. Please come this way.' Sister Jewell came out from behind the nursing station and, with Swannell in her wake, walked silently down the ward on rubber-soled shoes. 'We get one or two patients like this each year. It is the East End policing itself.' Sister Jewell spoke sniffily. 'I mean, as if the Health Service hasn't enough to do ... and isn't collapsing under bankruptcy. I confess, avoidable injuries and violence annoy me.' She progressed along the ward which had been arranged in the traditional 'Nightingale' style, with beds at equal intervals and abutting the walls on both sides at ninety degrees. A few patients had visitors. 'Open visiting hours,' Sister Jewell explained, as if reading Swannell's thoughts. 'It is a recently introduced system, a new development. I confess, freely so, that I prefer the old system of strictly enforced visiting hours but then I am now old enough to dislike any form of change, and I really do believe that things *were* better in the old days.' Swannell remained silent. He had long since learned not to argue with taxi drivers and nursing sisters, and his opinion of Sister Jewell as being a tyrant towards junior nurses was being reinforced by the second.

'In here.' Sister Jewell stopped outside the door of a private room, with painted wooden walls up to waist height and frosted glass up to a height of ten feet thereafter. The room had no ceiling. 'He was brought in last evening.' Sister Jewell continued to speak but with a lowered voice. The room offered privacy of vision but not sound. 'He was found on the pavement near here. There is not one square inch of flesh that is not bruised, and I mean one square inch ... from the soles of his feet to his scalp, yet not one bone in his body is broken and his teeth have been left intact. I confess that he could be mistaken for a gentleman of the subcontinent, but he is as Northern European as you and me.'

'I see.'

'Hence not wanting to distress the other patients. They get upset when they find out that such injury is caused by premeditated violence, rather than accident.'

'Yes ... I can understand that.' Swannell nodded. 'I did wonder but now I fully appreciate why you have isolated him.'

'Thank you. Well, as I said, I have seen the like. He was numb last night, wasn't feeling very much at all according to the nursing notes, but he woke in discomfort this morning. He refused breakfast and I confess that I doubt he'll partake of lunch. He will get more uncomfortable over the next few days, then the pain will stabilize, but it will remain for a long time. We'll put him on painkillers but he will still feel something.'

'How long before he is recovered?'

'Physically ... a few months, but mentally ... never ... the mental scars will never heal, they just don't ever heal.'

'Months!'

'Oh, yes ... months. He won't be here for that length of time, the pressure on beds won't permit it, but I have known such bruising to take six months to fade completely. He was probably the victim of a

305

sustained assault which lasted a full day.'
Sister Jewell shrugged. 'That's the East End.
Some of the trainees can't hack it and trans-
fer to the west London hospitals. It's not the
injury itself you see – it's the cause that
upsets them.'

'Yes.'

'Now he is brown all over, that will turn
into the mottled mix of blue-and-black
bruising, then he'll turn yellow as if he is
badly jaundiced, but once the bruising turns
yellow, then at least he is on the healing side
of things. But that will still take months.
He's in for a very uncomfortable summer ...
So that's gangland London, but you know
that as much as me – the East End policing
itself, like I said. He said he wanted to talk
to a Mr Brunnie.'

'He's busy. I am his senior officer.'

'Very well.' Sister Jewell opened the door
and led Swannell into the room. Victor
Swannell baulked at the sight which greeted
him, and he saw then that Sister Jewell was
not exaggerating when she said that even
though he was Northern European, Clive
'The Pox' Sherwin could be mistaken for an
Asian, such was the depth and extent of the
bruising. His eyes were swollen shut.

'Police to see you, Mr Sherwin.' Sister
Jewell spoke softly yet efficiently. There was

306

no sympathy in her voice. 'One gentleman, I have seen his identity card.'

'Mr Brunnie?' Sherwin asked weakly. 'I can't see nothing ... I can't ... nothing. I can make out it's day-time ... but nothing else.'

'No, it's Mr Swannell, Mr Brunnie is busy. He can't come but you can talk to me.'

'Well, I will leave you.' Sister Jewell turned and walked out of the room, closing the door silently behind her.

'I talked to Mr Brunnie.'

'Yes, I know, I read the recording of the chat you had. He made you an offer.'

'Yes, witness protection.'

'Indeed. The offer is still on the table.' Swannell drew up a chair and sat beside the bed.

'Yes ... Yates did this to me. I never said nothing, and he goes and does this. I'm seen as a grass now. No one gets a slap like this if they don't deserve it, so no one will believe me when I say I never grassed.' He choked. 'I'm finished ... finished ... I can't go no-where now so I need that protection offer.' He drew his breath deeply. 'Blimey ... and they tell me this isn't it; they tell me the pain will get worse before it gets better ... that this is only the start of it.'

'Sister told me the same thing.'

'She's a hard old girl. Met her for the first

307

time this morning when she came on duty. She said, "People who have had a heart attack need this bed", then walked out. I won't be leaving her a box of chocolates when I go.'

'So what do you want to tell me? What can you tell me? Witness protection comes at a price.'

'Everything ... everything I know about Curtis Yates and that cow Gail Bowling, she's the boss, not Yates – but they are partners ... he's a little bit junior to her ... and that import and export business – furniture! Do me a favour, it's ecstasy pills out and humans in ... girls mainly from Eastern Europe on their way to the massage parlours.'

'We thought as much.' Swannell took his notepad from his jacket pocket and pressed the top of his ballpoint. 'I'll get an overview to start with – all the details will come out later.'

'OK ... and I can tell you where the bodies are buried. I put them there.'

'Did you actually murder anyone, Clive?'

'No, but I was one of Yates's and Bowling's undertakers; I got rid of the bodies. Sometimes in cement in the basement of a renovated house in Kilburn, sometimes under a tree...'

'A tree?'

'A cherry tree; Yates likes them. He had his own take on "green burials" before they became fashionable with the save-the-planet brigade.' He winced with pain. 'I'll tell you everything ... everything ... but I need the full package ... new name, new address and a plod outside that door. Once Yates knows I'm grassing him up, my life's in danger.'

'Well, if you can tell us what you say you can tell us ... then that is guaranteed, Clive.'

'Clive.' The man winced again. 'Clive "The Pox" Sherwin ... that name belongs to the past ... well in the past ... ancient history.'

'OK, but for now I'll still call you Clive.' Swannell leaned slightly forward and spoke in a soft, gentle tone. 'The new name will come later.'

'Alright ... understand, dare say it took longer than a day to build Rome.'

'Is a good way of looking at it, Clive.' Swannell nodded. 'It is a good way to look at it.'

'Mind you, I'll keep Clive ... I just need a new surname.'

'I'm afraid you can't, it doesn't work like that.' Swannell glanced around him – the clinical whites and creams, the heavy grade industrial linoleum, the scent of disinfec-

309

tant, the sound of traffic outside the old Victorian era building. 'We have the names listed, you can't mix and match. We need to know which names have been taken, both Christian and surname.'

'I see.'

'Never know your luck though, Clive ... look down the old list and you'll likely see a "Clive" somebody, though you might not like the surname ... but it's a long list, doubtless there will be more than one "Clive" on it.'

'See what I see, when I see it ... when I can see. Now I know what it's like to be blind. They did a good job on me, Mr Swannell. I mean, did they go to town or did they go to town?'

'They went to town alright, Clive. So tell me what you can. We can start now ... see how far we get. I can come back as often as need be.'

'Bring some grapes.' Clive Sherwin forced a smile.

'I can do that.'

'OK, I'll sing like a canary, but first ... first...' He winced in discomfort. 'First off, you don't have a lot of time ... You sent a lassie in ... undercover ... a female officer. She was rumbled right from the start.'

'Yes, we thought as much. We don't know

where she is...'

'I do ... I have an idea where she might be ... don't know the old address.'

'Come on, Clive!' Swannell raised his voice. He heard it echo within the glass walls of the isolation ward.

'Her life's in danger.'

'If it isn't over already...' Again Sherwin winced.

'Clive! Don't faint on me ... not now.'

'I won't faint. Listen ... you need to drive north-west out of the Smoke ... up into Hertfordshire.'

'Yes.'

'I don't know the road...'

'That's a big help...'

'You have to drive out of Hemel Hempstead, out the other side from the Smoke. I don't know the road number but I am sure it's signposted to Leighton Buzzard.'

'Leighton Buzzard?'

'Sure of it. It's an A road, but just one lane in either direction. I only went there a couple of times. I'm doing my best ... there's a white cottage.'

'A white cottage?'

'Yes, old building ... got a date on it ... 1610 AD.'

'1610? You sure, Clive?'

'Certain. It's my birthday, see – sixteenth

October: 1610 – so I remembered it. When I first clocked it, I saw the date and I thought, "well, I never". Anyway, you turn opposite it up a farm track. It leads to a farm. It's got a thatched roof.'

'The farmhouse?'

'No, the cottage – white, with 1610 on it ... above the door.'

'Still a bit of a needle in a haystack, Clive.'

'You need to crack on. If she's still alive, she won't be soon. Curtis Yates has a thing about noon.'

'Noon?'

'Yes, he doesn't like chilling anyone before noon ... he really prefers the night-time ... but it's like deadline noon for him – after midday he starts cooling his victims.'

Swannell took out his mobile phone from his pocket and punched the keys. He stood as his call was answered and turned away from Sherwin. 'Boss, we need to move...'

Curtis Yates lit a cigar and smiled at Gail Bowling. 'I enjoyed that, a leisurely breakfast ... now a cigar ... and then a pleasant drive out to Hertfordshire.'

'Yes, I know what you mean.' Gail Bowling smiled. 'The cherry orchard keeps growing.'

Harry Vicary slammed his phone down, ran

from his office to the detective constables' office. 'Grab your coats,' he yelled to Frank Brunnie and Tom Ainsclough. 'I'll tell you what's happening on the way.'

'Where are we going, boss?'

'Out to Hemel Hempstead,' Vicary panted, 'other side of same. We'll have to phone the Hertfordshire police – we'll need some uniforms ... and local knowledge. We need to find a white cottage; out on the road to Leighton Buzzard ... dated 1610 apparently. Penny's there and in danger.'

'At the cottage?'

'No ... I'll explain in the car.' He turned and ran down the corridor.

'I hope we're in time.' Ainsclough ran behind him, followed by Brunnie.

'You hope we're in time!' Vicary replied angrily. 'You didn't send her there.'

Penny Yewdall stiffened at the sound of car tyres arriving and moving slowly over the rough surface of the farmyard. She heard the dog bark aggressively.

'They're here,' Billy Kemp whined. 'They-'ve come too early.'

'Early?' Penny Yewdall glanced at him. It was by then, she estimated, about noon. 'What do you mean, early?'

'Yates has this thing about killing during

the day. I told you, he doesn't like icing geezers until after dark. I thought we'd have a few hours yet. How do you think they are going to do it?'

The door of the barn opened and winter sunlight illuminated the interior; the rats were heard to scurry for the shadows. Billy Kemp cried out in panic.

Penny Yewdall did not know whether to laugh or cry, when, in the next instant, Harry Vicary stepped into the barn.

'Oh good.' Vicary smiled softly. 'I was very worried that we would be late.' Brunnie and Ainsclough stepped into the barn behind him; the officers spread out making sure the building was clear of felons.

Yewdall blinked against the sudden rush of light. 'How...?'

Harry Vicary held up his hand, 'All in good time ... but for now let's just say that Victor Swannell met a man who told him where we were likely to find you. He gave excellent directions ... turn right at a white cottage dated 1610 AD. We could hardly miss. He told Swannell about a row of cherry trees...'

'Yes, they're just outside behind the barn. I'll show you. Where is Yates?'

'He's being arrested. Gail Bowling as well. We have officers going to their house in

Virginia Water. It's all over, Penny. The nightmare is over.'

Later that same year, as the sun sank over fields of freshly baled wheat in north Norfolk, a man and a woman, walking arm in arm, returned from their stroll and entered the village in which stood their hotel. They entered the bar of the hotel and each had a glass of orange juice; they then went to the restaurant of the hotel and were directed to a table for two. They had agreed upon an early dinner before retiring for an early night.

'Well,' the man said, 'as I was telling you, they all started collapsing to save what they could of themselves, and each privately vowing to kill Clive "The Pox" Sherwin for being the first one to squeal, but Henry Packer, the guardian of the farm in Hertfordshire, saw the opportunity to save himself and, like Sherwin, he too is living under a new name somewhere north of Watford. The principal players collected life: Yates, Bowling and 'Rusher' Boyd. Lesser players like Sonya Clements and Felicity Skidmore got lesser sentences, and Josie Pinder went back to the North of England to complete her studies. She had her eyes well-opened and realized that Salford isn't such a bad place after all.'

'Their property?' The woman studied the menu.

'Oh, confiscated,' the man replied without looking up from his copy of the menu, 'all of it has been seized under the proceeds of crime legislation. So if they do come out of prison at some far distant point, then they will come out to the dole queues and hostel living. Quite a fall from grace.'

'And others got closure?'

'Yes, that is the pleasing thing. Mr Halkier can now visit his daughter's grave, and Mr O'Shea can now visit his wife's grave. Victor Swannell found out what happened to Charlotte Varney, who disappeared some years ago and who was linked to Curtis Yates. It was one of his cold cases you see.'

'Ah...'

'And a girl called Jennifer Reeves, an early victim – her remains and the remains of Charlotte Varney being found under a cherry tree ... and of course their relatives now also have closure. Tragic that they lost their daughters in that way, but at least they now know what happened ... it is some comfort, some little comfort.'

The couple stopped talking and leaned back in their chairs as a waiter wearing a starched white tunic approached their table.

'Would you like to see the wine list, sir?' he asked pleasantly.

'No, thank you,' Harry Vicary replied. 'Just a pitcher of chilled water for us both, please.'

'Water...' The youthful waiter scowled. 'Water? Yes, sir.'

'Restaurants only make money on their alcohol sales,' Vicary explained to his wife when the waiter had departed. 'The profit from food sales is slim to zero.'

'So we won't be popular customers?' Kathleen Vicary smiled.

'Nope, but we are paying through the nose for our room if you ask me. We could get cheaper in London. Mind you, they don't call this part of Norfolk "Chelsea North" for nothing.'

'Yes, can't help but notice the cars; our little VW next to those Ferraris. So, it is all wrapped up? Case closed?'

'Yes.' Vicary smiled. 'All wrapped up, all done and dusted. A whole criminal empire we hardly knew existed brought down in a matter of days, because a man chose to commit suicide by lying down in the snow right on top of a shallow grave he had dug some ten years earlier.'